THE IRISH ARRANGEMENT

LEONA WHITE

Copyright © 2024 by Leona White

All rights reserved.

No part of this book may be reproduced in any form or by any electronic or mechanical means, including information storage and retrieval systems, without written permission from the author, except for the use of brief quotations in a book review.

❦ Created with Vellum

BLURB

Arranged to marry, forced to stay...

CARA

Life has never been easy, but it's been even harder since mom got sick. Living on our farm and taking care of Mom's medical bills has left me desperate for money.

When my estranged father suggests I marry an Irish kingpin, I know I have no choice - especially with the promise of having Mom's bills paid off.

But I have a secret I'm keeping from my fiancé, Declan Sullivan - I can't get pregnant.

So I make him a deal: if I'm not pregnant six months into the marriage, he has to let me go.

But will he?

DECLAN

I made a promise to my father on his deathbed: that I would marry, and have an heir.

Cara Gallagher is much younger, tiny, and beautiful - but also breakable. She can't handle a man like me. But neither of us has a choice in the matter.

Especially once I meet the gorgeous little raven-haired beauty and start to crave more and more of her innocence…

Whatever she thinks, my ring is never leaving her finger. She's mine to keep…

And mine to break.

★ *Fall in love with this darkly addictive mafia kingpin & his inexperienced petite Irish rose! Read for FREE with your Kindle Unlimited subscription* ★

1

DECLAN

Blood flew out of the man's mouth as his head whipped back from my hit. The jab was hard and fast, sending him staggering to one knee. He wasn't done, though, struggling to stay on his two feet before the arc of my other hand could connect with his side.

A crack was my reward. His whoosh of a rough exhale was better yet. Best of all was his drop to the sweat-slicked floor of the fighting ring.

Take that, you fucker.

Heaving in air to catch my breath, I stood braced and alert in case this fight the Boyles sponsored would stand again. If he wanted more, if he was eager to literally fight to the death, then by all means, I was here for it.

In the distance, outside this ring where I'd defeated countless fighters and trained even more, I noticed the spectators grimacing and scowling. This wasn't a match for the crowds. We were settling a personal matter here, and I'd be damned if anyone from the Boyles would think to suggest any of my men cheated.

"What's that now?" I taunted, wiping my hand over my mouth. My lips weren't split like the exhausted and beaten man at my feet. He had yet to get up. Braced on his side, curling into his tenderest injuries I'd given him, he surrendered.

"You want to go around telling everyone the Sullivans are liars?" I growled, climbing through the ring's ropes.

The Boyle shook his head, nudging his companion that they should go. "Come on. Let's get out of here."

I grunted a mirthless laugh as I accepted a towel from my brother, Ian, who also stood by watching. As I walked further from the ring to approach the two men affiliated with the Boyle Family, I cocked my head to the side.

"Nothing to say?"

Peter Boyle smirked at me, his dark glare full of loathing and disdain. We'd never gotten along with our rivals, but over time, the Sullivans had learned to keep their distance, and the Boyles knew not to mess with us either. Except last week, when Peter claimed that one of my fighters cheated in the ring and his man—lying on the ring's floor and panting to survive—should've won that fight.

"Fuck you, Dec." Peter shook his head, walking out with his lackey.

"Hey!" Ian called out, grinning as he watched them go. "You forgot your trash."

Peter didn't stop, leaving and grumbling.

"Stupid motherfucker," I muttered, wiping my face and making sure those two left without bothering anyone else here. The sounds of men training resumed, and the usual bustle of the large gym returned to normal. The Sullivan Clan dabbled in all sorts of avenues of income. My family had risen to wealth and prominence hundreds of years ago with the success of many illegal and dangerous businesses, but I preferred this one. Fighting. If I wasn't training them, I participated in matches myself, and I took it personally when the Boyles disparaged my reputation. All of the men who fought under the Sullivan name did so honestly. We stood by our strength and honor, and I'd punish anyone who tried to cut corners and cheat.

"Let's see them try to accuse one of us again," Ian said.

I nodded, glancing at him again. He wasn't a blood relation, only an adopted sibling, but he'd always been my right-hand man. In a finely tailored suit, he looked out of place here. This gritty, loud, and violence-prone warehouse was a far cry from his office in the city. I cut a sharp contrast, sweaty and down to my pants from that fight.

"What brings you by?" Ian and I were close, but he handled a lot of administrative things for my father, the leader of our Clan. It wasn't often that he stopped over here, unless it was the night of a big fight. I squinted at him through the sting of sweat dripping into my eyes as I unwrapped my hands.

"Dad." He lost all residue of his smirk at the Boyles. Lines etched on his face, tugging his expression down with a sober frown. "He's not doing well."

"Tell me something I don't know." I huffed. "He hasn't been doing well for years." Donal Sullivan was a larger-than-life sort of Irishman no one would dare to disrespect, but for the last ten years, his pulmonary conditions had worsened gravely. His body failed him faster with every passing day, and I dreaded the idea of his being gone soon.

Ian shook his head, stuffing his hands in his pockets. "No. He's even worse. Riley called and told me that the doctors have been to the estate three times this week."

Fuck. I wiped the towel over my face once more. My duties kept me in the city. It wasn't often that I could hang out at the massive family home where Dad stayed, usually bedridden and trying to tolerate a moderate level of activity. I hadn't been home since last weekend, and I could take Ian and Riley's word as the truth.

"It's got to be bad if she's calling," Ian said, raising his brows.

"I know." Donal Sullivan was a proud man, and he'd ordered his primary doctor to downplay the severity of his status. Ian and I often felt like we didn't have the whole picture of how near our father was to his deathbed. They glossed over facts and no longer contacted us with worries about Dad's decline. If Riley, one of the cooks, also Ian's longtime lover, took it upon herself to break that rule and update Ian about Dad's health, it had to be bad.

"I'll head out there." I sighed, tossing the towel to the bin where they were collected. After I grabbed a quick shower, I'd drive straight there.

Ian walked alongside me, also scoping out the activity of the other men training and exercising here. "I'll wait for you. We may as well ride together."

"Yeah." Because if both of us were there to check on him, he'd have a harder time dismissing us.

An hour later, we entered the estate house and hurried up to Dad's wing. I doubted he'd left his bed for at least a couple of weeks. He'd be in the same position, with the same sour and gruff temperament, as he had the last time I saw him.

Yet, I wasn't prepared for how much he'd worsened. He was barely able to breathe, gaunt and thinner.

"Dad," I greeted somberly. I didn't check my tone, though, and it came out sounding like a scolding.

"How bad is it?" Ian said as he approached the bed with me.

Riley glanced at us, her brows raised, and backed out of the room with the tray of an untouched dinner.

"How bad is it?" Dad growled. "I'm dying. What do you expect?"

He'd been saying that for years.

"You don't look well," I commented as neutrally as possible.

"Looks like you need to check a mirror too," he shot back, spry in his attitude. He thumbed his chin, indicating where I'd taken a hard hit from the Boyles' fighter earlier.

I shrugged, glancing at the oxygen tank positioned near the head of the bed. Like usual, the thin, clear hose was lying on the mattress. The plastic nose piece rested, unused.

You stubborn, spiteful man.

Ian picked it up and held it out, but Dad swatted his offer away. "Ah, don't mess with that. What good would it do?"

"It'd help you breathe, for one thing," Ian replied as he dutifully gave up and released the hose. We were both too used to him to ever push hard. What Donal Sullivan wanted, he got.

"Why make me suffer any longer?" He huffed a laugh, which turned into coughing and wheezing. "At this rate, I'd be asking you to put me out of my misery."

Ian and I shared a look. He'd voiced the very thing both of us dreaded. If Dad ever asked us to do that, we'd struggle with obeying him in such a final wish. We didn't want to lose him, but we understood how miserable he had to be.

"But it's too soon. I'll fucking die knowing you don't have an heir."

I rolled my eyes, dropping to sit on the bed.

"I can't," Dad insisted. "I can't die until you have an heir. I refuse to go to the grave knowing our line, our family, will die out with you."

Ian bit his lip and stuck his hands in his pockets again, his usual stance when he was uncomfortable about something. "It's not like he hasn't tried."

"Oh, bullshit," Dad argued.

But I did. I had tried. Twice.

"I don't see you married right now," he said, narrowing his light-blue eyes at me.

I opened and closed my mouth. At a loss for words, I struggled with figuring out how long I had to put that task off.

"Finding him a wife is, uh, easier said than done," Ian quipped.

I shot him a look of annoyance. "Hey, you could always knock someone up too."

He laughed as Dad shook his head. "I refuse to die until I know you've secured an heir to the Sullivan name, the Sullivan bloodline."

Ian shrugged at me, nonplussed. It was common knowledge that he couldn't be expected to satisfy Dad's request. Not only was he younger than me, but he was also not a blood brother. I was the only one. The only son.

"It's always been like that," Dad argued. "I didn't make the rules, but you have to produce an heir, Declan."

And through marriage. I was always careful to glove up when fucking a woman. The last thing we needed was an illegitimate child to pay for and raise. And I didn't welcome the headache of a gold-digging woman to get knocked up by me and expect money, either.

"You have to find someone," Dad insisted.

"You think I haven't tried?" I stood and crossed my arms. "I married Erin."

He sneered. "Who fucked one of those Italians. Only she had to have an affair with one who had a jealous wife."

Erin was my first attempt at marriage and getting an heir. That Italian lover killed her to erase his evidence of infidelity.

"And Caitlin…" I shook my head. My second wife killed herself. She was too soft, too traumatized, she'd warned, from living with a "monster" like me.

"You need to find a fucking wife who can last long enough to give you a child." Dad sighed, slumping back to his pillows. This argument wasn't anything new, and each time he implored me to get this taken care of, he was tired of the wait and had lost hope.

Ian cleared his throat. "I've been trying to look around and find someone."

I rolled my eyes. My brother playing match-maker. It was ridiculous.

"But not many Families want their daughters to marry him."

Dad and I stared at each other. "He's a fine man. He represents the future of the Sullivan name. The next leader."

"But he's also ruthless, prone to being brutish, and very impatient," Ian said.

"Losing two wives can't instill much faith," I admitted.

"Have you asked the Murrays?" Dad raised his bushy gray brows, looking from Ian to me.

I didn't give a shit about finding a wife. Even though I understood what Dad expected of me, I was fine with Ian trying—and failing—to secure me a bride who'd stick around.

"Shane Murray?" Ian asked, rubbing his chin. "No, I haven't."

"He's got a daughter." Dad nodded. "Saoirse, I think her name was. Young, but she's got to be of age by now."

"What makes you think Shane would want to offer her up?" I asked. I hardly cared who she was or what she looked like. If she had a pussy I could fuck, then that was all that mattered. It wasn't like I'd actually be a husband and spend time with her. I had too much shit to do, and once Dad passed, I'd be completely in charge.

"He won't want to," Ian said. "Every single Family I've contacted, it's a unanimous rejection."

I smirked at him. "Thanks for the vote of confidence."

"Just telling it like it is."

"I helped Shane Murray years ago. He benefited from the Sullivan protection, and he's never paid back the debt."

Now I was intrigued. Maybe this would be the best solution.

"You reach out to Shane Murray," he told us, "and tell him that he owes me. He owes us a significant sum that he'll never be able to repay if he lived another hundred years." Coughing broke up his speech, but he managed to finish after a moment. "Demand that he offer Saoirse in marriage in exchange for his debt."

I stood, nodding. Saoirse Sullivan. I would make it happen. "I'll contact him right now." Ian could handle this chore of correspondence, but I may as well live up to my reputation as a rough, hard asshole every father feared their daughter would meet. If Shane needed some encouragement to go along with this payment plan, it'd be my pleasure to get it done.

Whatever it took. Dad didn't have much time left with how blue his lips looked and how weak he was to sit upright in bed.

I'd get him a damn heir as soon as possible.

2

CARA

Flies buzzed ahead, and I flapped my work glove to dismiss them as I hurried out of the stables. If I wanted these people at the hospital to take me and my calls seriously, I'd have better luck having this conversation away from the sheep and horses. Bleating and whinnying animals didn't bother me any, but I doubted this woman from the city would agree.

"Listen. I understand you want me to be patient and wait for—"

The woman on the other line sighed. "No. *You* listen, Miss Gallagher. I've explained this several times. The policy states that if you miss an appointment—"

I slapped my gloves to my dusty jeans, gritting my teeth. "But she didn't! My mother didn't miss her appointment."

"From my end of things, it looks like she did."

"No." I shook my head, catching a look from the only stable hand we could still afford to employ here at my mother's work farm. Oscar raised his brows, sticking his pitchfork in the hay pile he was transferring, and watched as I paced out here in the open. I wasn't sure what

I'd ever do without the older man. He helped me keep this place in operation, and it was all I had. All my mother ever had. Nora Gallagher didn't contribute much to the place she got from her parents, but I gave it my all.

"She did not miss her appointment. A man from your office called the night before and said that she had to move her appointment time to three o'clock on the twelfth, not eleven. And that's what we showed up for."

"Did you receive a confirmation email of this supposed appointment?" she asked.

Supposed. I held in a growl of frustration. "Yes. For the original one at eleven, which we confirmed. *He* called and changed it after we'd confirmed the first one."

"That change doesn't show up on our end." She cleared her throat as the sound of tapping keys came through the line. "So, according to me, that request for a change didn't happen."

I threw my gloves down on a tree stump. "Let me get this straight. According to *you*, I'm lying now? This is *your* mistake."

"I made no such mistake."

"Fine. Someone in your office did."

"I see no record of that."

"Want proof?" I snarled. "I have my call log. Someone named Chad called from your office and asked us to change our appointments due to a doctor's conflict. I don't have all day to sit around and accept these last-minute changes, but it just so happened that we could swing it that day. And now you expect me to understand that this is somehow *my* fault. Or that I'm making this shit up. So that my mother won't be seen by her specialist for two more months? We waited five months to even get *this* appointment."

She huffed. "And if your mother had shown up at her appointment time of eleven on the twelfth, she would have seen her specialist as desired."

Desired? Who ever wanted to need a specialist on their medical case? No one. That was who. My mother never wished for any of this, a stubborn bout of cancer that kept returning. An autoimmune disease. An infection from a negligent cook at a restaurant. She never desired any of this, but it was her lot in her unfortunate life. It was my headache to deal with the best I could. Losing my cool with this receptionist wasn't my finest moment, but for God's sake. How much stress could a person take before snapping?

"I refuse to accept this change. Ask your staff. Speak to Chad. I don't care if it wasn't documented on your end. It was on *mine*."

"I'm afraid that's not possible."

I narrowed my eyes. "And why the hell not?"

"Chad is unavailable at the moment."

I pulled the phone away, covered the mouthpiece, and yelled. Riled up and heaving for air, I returned. "I don't give a shit. You are not going to make my mother wait two more months for an appointment that your office screwed up on."

"We do not tolerate this kind of behavior," she retorted sassily.

"Oh, but incompetent employees get a free pass at the expense of the patients?"

She huffed. "I have nothing further to say to you other than a reminder that you will be billed an additional missed-appointment fee for not showing up. Goodbye."

At the beep of the call disconnecting, I gripped my phone so hard that I swore I'd crack the case.

"I hate you!" I bellowed it, knowing Mom was asleep on the other side of the house. I'd never wake her from a nap, but I had to vent somehow. If it wasn't scrambling to get her to her appointments in the city while not slacking on the farm, it was hunting down available doses of her medications. Plural, because she required a variety of drugs to keep her as healthy and pain-free as possible.

"Cara..." Oscar approached me carefully. He was a staple around here and always had been. I'd grown up under his wing, learning how to work on this farm. I wouldn't lash out on him, but I detested his trying to talk to me right now.

"We can try to shift some things around and make sure you don't struggle with getting Nora to her appointments."

Oh, my God. Why was everyone glossing over the fact that it wasn't my fault? Why couldn't he understand that I had shifted my chores to get her there on time? And it was *their* fault for playing around with me like this.

"It's not that, Oscar," I warned. "They're claiming it's just some office SNAFU. I always make time for Nora's care." It added up. Doctor appointments. Bloodwork. Dialysis until she could get a kidney transplant. Therapy. More appointments to check on her medications. The list went on and on, but I'd never failed her. I couldn't. I was all she had in this world. Me and this farm that kept a few dollars in her bank account after things were all said and done.

"All right, but I'm just saying..." He shrugged, almost sheepish. "We could sell off some of the land and have a little cushion for these sorts of things. And if you sell the second tractor, maybe it could cover the pay for a second pair of hands around here."

I hung my head. He had to bring *that* up again. Oscar and I never saw eye to eye on every decision, but he didn't get it. I had to be this frugal to save up for Mom to get that kidney transplant, if and when she would be matched. He didn't see the bank statements like I did.

Already exhausted from dealing with the woman at the specialist's office, I felt zero energy for round three or four of hashing out why I wouldn't agree with Oscar's suggestions. It sounded good on paper, but he didn't have the whole picture. Trusting Oscar with the farm was one matter. Bringing him in to see how much debt Nora had incurred just to stay alive was another matter I would not welcome him to learn about.

Some days, it took all I had to keep us afloat. Today was another one of those rotten ones where I couldn't tell whether I was drowning yet or not.

"Hiring another stable hand would help bring in more, ya know?" he said, propping his hands on his hips. "More work to be done and more income when we got more sheep to sell."

I shook my head. *I don't have the freedom to invest like that.*

"And with you taking off so often…" He winced. "It's a lot on my shoulders, picking up your slack."

I grabbed my gloves and glowered at him. "I'm not 'taking off'."

"I don't mean it like that." He hurried to follow after me as I returned to the bigger barn.

"I'm not slacking," I bit out. How dare he even think to say it like that? I busted my ass to keep this farm running, to get Mom to her appointments. Every morning I woke up, I wished to escape it all. And every night when I lay in bed, my body worn and fatigued from the manual labor, I prayed that I could have another option in my life. Any other option. For an end to all this stress and toiling away with the last fiber of my being.

"Cara!" Oscar hustled to keep up with me. "I ain't meaning anything nasty like that. But it's a lot. When you're not here, it's not easy to keep up. This farm is a lot for one person. It's a lot for two."

"I don't know what to tell you," I replied, pausing at the fence where the sheep needed shearing. "This is what it is. And I'm not going to waste more time arguing with you. So long as the sun's shining, I'll do what I can and hope it's enough."

He pursed his lips, eyeing me as I opened the door to the stall and let the wooden panel slam shut at him.

My phone rang as I reached for the clippers, and I dropped my head back and groaned. I'd jinxed myself. Because if that was that office calling again, or anyone else hounding after me for money or appointment changes, or who knew what else, I'd lose all the waking hours today had for me.

Spotting an unfamiliar number on the screen, I answered. "Hello?"

"Cara Gallagher?"

I exhaled a long breath and waved at the flies. "Who's asking?"

"I'm calling on behalf of Shane Murray," the prim voice said.

I rolled my eyes and grinned, feeling like a maniac. "Oh, sure. A friendly call from my father." I hadn't heard from him since I was five. "And what does *he* want, huh? Since I clearly shouldn't plan on getting any work done today." I set my boot on the railing to the fence. "Go on, city boy. Enlighten me. Tell me what message my estranged, worthless father might want to share with me so I can accomplish nothing for this day's work. Go on. Don't be shy."

He cleared his throat, not giving me the satisfaction of remarking on my sarcastic tone. "The Murray Family would like to offer a total and full payment for Nora Gallagher's outstanding debt and medical bills."

I froze, ignoring the bleating sheep, whinnying horses, and buzzing flies. My focus zeroed in on what this stuffy man said.

Full payment? Just like that?

"I'm listening." I didn't bother wasting my anger on the fact that my father would've snooped and investigated our lives to even know that Mom had debts. At the same time, I refused to be this gullible.

There's a catch. I know there is.

"And the Murray Family would also like to extend an offer to see to the coverage of Nora Gallagher's continued medical care. *Private* care," he added with emphasis.

Private, meaning not as long of a wait.

I narrowed my eyes, on edge for this out-of-the-blue call. The man couldn't even call himself. He had an assistant do it. "Out of the goodness of his heart, huh?"

"No."

I raised my brows, surprised that he'd be honest about that.

"Mr. and Mrs. Murray would like to invite you to speak with them about this arrangement."

Another trip away from the farm. Oscar would bitch about my 'taking off' again, but I wondered if this could be worth my while. While I was guarded and skeptical, I considered looking into it. After all, what the hell could my so-called father want from me that would be so bad?

"When?"

"The Murrays would like to consult with you tomorrow."

The Murrays. It sounded so formal. Official. Like they were strangers —and he was one. Shane Murray knocked up my mother and ran. He'd run straight into Keira's arms and stuck with her when I was just a toddler. While I was the unwanted and tossed-aside daughter born of the woman he hadn't wanted to stand by, my stepmother and stepsister formed a "real" family with my sperm donor.

"*Tomorrow!*"

LEONA WHITE

For fuck's sake. I rubbed my brow, thinking through the list of things to get done before the next day.

My phone beeped with an incoming email. "Hold, please."

I muted the call and glanced at the incoming message.

It was another reminder of the fees to secure a place on the waitlist for Mom's surgery.

Feeling trapped, I sighed and resumed the call.

"Fine. I'll see them tomorrow."

3

DECLAN

Right after Ian and I spoke with Dad, I contacted Shane Murray. He answered, confused about the direct call. His first stupid reply was why I hadn't gone through his assistant, as though I were some plebeian who had to go through channels to reach a self-important asshole like Shane.

Then, once I identified myself, he wizened up to a proper degree of fear that I was reaching out to him at all.

When I told him under no uncertain terms that I expected Saoirse as my bride in exchange for his debt, he reverted to shock.

He hemmed and hawed, too stunned to answer with the obvious right answer to my demands, that of, *yes, Mr. Sullivan, I will tell my daughter to prepare to marry you within the week*. Instead, when I dictated that I wanted arrangements agreed upon within one day, he'd alternated between clamming up and stuttering, saying he'd have his "people" get back with my "people" to iron out the details.

That was forty-eight hours ago.

As if he could count on dealing with anyone but me. Ian pinned down one of the doctors who said he estimated that Dad would live for maybe a few more months at the most.

Time was of the essence. I wasn't going to wait around for Shane's "people" to contact my staff. It was time to escalate to a man-to-man understanding.

I would prove my father wrong. He would *not* die without knowing an heir stood in line to take over the Family after me.

Ian looked me up and down, inspecting my appearance as he waited near his car. I didn't need him to come along, but having backup never hurt. I'd found that Ian could speak more diplomatically than me, anyway.

His lips twitched, but he didn't share his thoughts.

"What?" I furrowed my brow, glancing at myself.

"You clean up… nice."

"Shut up." I *did* clean up nice. Not a spot of blood showed on my hands for once. I couldn't do anything for the bruises, and I wouldn't try, anyway.

"You could try smiling," he suggested as we got in the car.

"Fuck off." I sighed, closing my eyes for a moment as I tried to relax in the passenger seat. Last night, I'd slept like shit, and I felt every bit of my almost forty years today.

"I'm just saying," he replied good-naturedly, used to taking shit from me. "If you're going to meet your bride now, it wouldn't hurt to *look* friendly."

"I won't be friends with my wife," I deadpanned. All I needed her for was to pop out a baby.

"Try not to scare this one off *before* you marry."

I shook my head. "Funny."

"Do you think he'll try to back out of the deal?" he asked, serious now as he drove toward the Murrays' home.

"No." I sat up, smoothing down my jacket. "He didn't actually tell me *yes* yet." Nor did he say *no*, which I would cling to. "I think my call came as a surprise, and in the shock of the moment, he didn't know what to say."

Ian grunted a single laugh. "But he's dealt with Dad before."

"Twenty years ago."

"Regardless, he should know that nobody tells a Sullivan *no*."

"Agreed." Which was why I planned to reiterate that in person now. Shane Murray was a small-time imbecile with so much arrogance, he stuffed his ego to the brim. He wouldn't feel important or be cocky when we spoke in person. Even if I surprised him by just showing up here now, he'd understand that he had no grounds to turn my offer down.

I'd looked back in the records. Shane owed a shit-ton of money to us, and he hadn't paid up a single penny.

"Ready?" Ian asked when we arrived several minutes later.

I shot him a side-eyed look of annoyance. "You mean is *he* ready?" I wasn't worried. I had no reason to be anxious about making my demands realized more clearly in person.

Ian smiled. "We know he won't be ready," he said as we walked up to the door.

I hadn't announced my visit, but since I'd called him, he had to be sweating and nervous. Especially when he'd had the gall to cease communications.

Ian lifted his finger toward the bell, but I beat him to it, pounding my fist on the front door. He smirked at me dully, and I shrugged. "This isn't a fucking polite afternoon tea, Brother."

"No, it won't be."

A portly butler opened the door, trying and failing to look regal. The flash of alarm in his eyes was the first clue that he knew who I was.

"Where's Murray?" I said, plowing past him.

"Oh—I—Sir—Wait—" He stumbled over his exclamations, jogging after me. Ian chuckled, keeping up the rear, and I hoped at least he was having fun.

"Murray?" I hollered.

"What on *earth* is all this—" The woman speaking stopped short as she entered the front foyer. Her heels clicked one last time on the polished marble floor. Dressed in a beige pantsuit, formal and too stiff on her unshapely frame, she gawked at me. "Who..." She clamped her lips shut as her eyes opened wider.

The shock in her eyes felt like a reward. The fear that quickly replaced it boosted my spirits. "Where's Murray?" I demanded.

"You can't... You are not permitted to simply enter my home and make demands like this."

I stalked over to her until her pungent perfume irritated my nose. Towering over her, I bothered with another once-over. Plastic, taut, and tense. Snappy, but not so confident to stand up tall when I glowered down my nose at her.

"I can do whatever the fuck I want."

"Dec." Ian sighed. "Perhaps it might go over better if you introduce yourself to your bride's mother before you terrify her."

Her lips pressed tighter together. Ire and determination burned in her gaze. "You will *never* marry my daughter."

I turned, scoffing at Ian. "Huh. Looks like they do want to try to tell me no, after all."

"No, no. That's not… No. Keira, please, let me handle this," Shane Murray said as he rushed down the stairs. Glancing at me facing off with his wife, he tried to smile. The expression didn't last. As he stepped down to the floor, he looked like he was about to piss himself. "Dec. My man."

"Don't fucking cozy up to me. It's Mr. Sullivan."

"Right. Right. Uh, Mr. Sullivan." He hustled closer, gripping Keira's arm to pull her back.

She wrenched free, glaring at her husband. "He is not—"

"Shh! Shh." He forced a chuckle, waving at her to quiet. "We'll discuss this matter like men. If you'd please, Mr. Sullivan. I've been looking forward to your visit." Smiling quickly but weakly, he gestured for me to enter the parlor with him.

"Like hell you've been looking forward to this meeting." I narrowed my eyes at him. "You were hoping to never hear from me again."

"Like *men*?" Keira exclaimed before we walked any further. "No. Absolutely not." She marched after us, tossing a look of disdain at Ian as he joined us. "I will not allow you," she scolded. "I don't trust you to speak for Saoirse."

I huffed, crossing my arms near the sofa Murray directed me to. "Who wears the pants here, so I know which one of you to address?"

Murray mumbled, unsure of what to say as Ian sat. Again, he gestured for me to sit. "If you'd please, Declan."

I lowered to the stiff, uncomfortable sofa facing the one he sat on. Keira lowered next to him, back straight and eyes beady on me.

"Mr. Sullivan, the answer is no," she said. "You will not marry my daughter."

"*Your* daughter?" Ian asked, raising his brows at her, then Shane. "Not his?"

A framed photo on the side table distracted me. The slim brunette smirked in her pose for the camera, and I wondered if that stuck-up bitch was Saoirse. She looked rigid, too skinny, like she'd break if I fucked her hard. I could already hear the whining a woman like that would make. And those fake breasts. God. Would it be too much to ask for a *real* woman? One with meat on her bones, someone who could stand up to a good pounding? And real tits to hold?

Keira tipped her nose up, noticing where I looked. She got up and hugged the frame to her as she sat again. "Saoirse will not marry *you* in exchange for any supposed, outdated debt." She sniffed. "You've probably fabricated it all."

I locked my stare on Shane, who fidgeted in his seat, avoiding any eye contact with me. Then I returned my glare to her. "Are you accusing me of lying?" I growled.

She didn't budge, seeming to hold her breath as she clutched the picture frame like it could be a shield.

"No!" Shane chuckled uneasily with that outburst. "No, no, Declan."

"Mr. Sullivan," I bit out.

"No, Mr. Sullivan. She's not *accusing* you of lying. No, not at all." He patted her forearm until she wrenched it away from his reach. "She just doesn't remember. It was so long ago. And you know, women." He huffed. "They don't know the details of business and all."

"Then you *are* aware that you owe the Sullivan Clan a significant sum." Ian produced a printout from his inner jacket pocket, set it on the coffee table between the sofas, and spun it with his finger for the couple to see.

Keira's eyes nearly bugged out. Shane winced. "Uh, the number's a little higher than what *I* recall, but, yeah…"

"Consider yourself fortunate that my father never decided to inflate the interest after all this time. You haven't paid a single cent back. But with your agreement that you'll arrange a wedding within one week, uniting me and your daughter in marriage, I will wipe the slate clean."

Keira let out a whine. "No." Now she gripped Shane's forearm, digging her manicured nails into his sleeve so hard that it might tear the fabric. "No, Mr. Sullivan. You *must* consider someone else for marriage."

Ian chuckled lightly. "We've considered any and everyone possible."

Shut the fuck up. It was already clear that this mother didn't want her bratty-looking daughter hitched with me. Ian didn't need to worsen my image by explaining that Saoirse was my last option.

"Not *my* daughter," she begged.

"Murray." I stood and held up the paper in his face. "Shall I collect on this amount now? Or will there be a fucking wedding at the end of this week?"

He swallowed, his Adam's apple bobbing. "Yes." He winced at Keira's tightened clutch on his forearm, trying to remove himself from her grip. "Yes. We will arrange for a wedding."

Ian stood, nodding once in acknowledgment. "Then we'll be in touch."

I maintained a level glare on them until I followed Ian out. We didn't mess with the butler, who wasn't even there anymore. He'd probably shat his pants with how we'd frightened him at the door and let ourselves in.

But we didn't leave. Ian glanced around, tipping his head toward the side of the house. I furrowed my brow and followed him, catching on to the fact that he wanted to listen to Keira and Shane. Their shouting match wasn't hard to eavesdrop on. With the windows open and both of their voices raised, we idled on the front sidewalk and heard it all while we lingered.

"You are out of your mind if you think we'll arrange for a wedding," she shouted.

"I think we have to," Shane whined.

"No. We won't. Not like this!" she threatened before the sounds of her heels clacked. A door slammed inside, and Shane groaned.

Ian and I walked back to his car. Once we were in, I let the tension of irritation and impatience bleed out of me with a deep exhale. "If they don't cooperate," I promised, "I'll fucking ruin them."

Ian nodded, setting the car in drive and pulling away. "Damn straight, we will, Brother."

4

CARA

I didn't know what to expect when I made the drive to see my father.

Shane Murray may as well have lived in a whole different world from me. I hadn't seen him in years, and the last time I did spot him, he'd treated me like scum he didn't want to be associated with. That was from my perspective as a child then, and now, at twenty-two years old, I was even wearier.

Being unwanted set a lot of things in stone. I was an outsider, invited to his lavish home. The butler seemed like a joke, as did all the gaudy ornamentations and décor. The chandelier dripped with more gems and crystals than I could ever imagine. My first thought as I stepped over the threshold was how much of a pain it would be to clean all these fine possessions set out for guests to notice and identify this residence as somewhere that money bled freely from wallets.

Silly me. They've got a crew. An army, a legion of peons to do the grunt work. Shane never had to lift his hand. My stepmother never cooked or kept the house. And Saoirse? She had to be an entitled, selfish brat by now.

I ignored the showy entrance, though, walking in after the pot-bellied butler. He huffed and puffed, clearly not a fan of cardio as he led me further into the house, past what looked like a parlor. Instead of bringing me to a room to receive guests for entertainment, he brought me to my father's study.

He sat there, looking older than what I remembered. I'd never cared to keep in touch with them, but I saw things online from time to time. Saoirse loved to be in the spotlight, and I supposed she considered herself an influencer on social media. Or maybe she was trying to be a model. I didn't remember, and I didn't care.

"What do you want?" I crossed my arms and ignored the butler leaving me in the grand study. Tall windows let in the fading light from the sunset, but ample lamps shone brightly.

Keira was the first to turn around. My stepmother stood there with my father, poring over something on a table at the wall behind the desk. As she turned to face me, she showed me how she'd aged too. Flatter, more weight, no curves. She'd always been a homely sort of woman, but that never stopped her from relying on cosmetic surgery to suffuse some appeal into her appearance.

And it still fails.

"About time *you* showed up," she sneered.

My father turned as well. His brows jumped up in surprise as he looked me over, almost as though he hadn't counted on me to come at all. "Oh."

"What do you want?" I wasn't here to play any games.

Keira rounded the desk, keeping her chin up and that regal attitude consistent. With all those facial lifts, her face didn't move much. She looked like a molded doll frowning without showing any lines. "That's how you greet us? Where are your manners?" She smirked. "Where is your sense of propriety?" Even though her face was frozen, I saw how little she thought of me.

In jeans and a plain T-shirt, I was comfortable and true to myself. I'd brushed my ponytail before I'd come, and I had to be mostly clean. Mud lined the edges of my boots. Or maybe it was manure. I didn't care either way. What they saw was what they'd get—a hardworking woman busting her ass to keep her mother alive and her family business from failing.

"I don't care about being proper or having manners. I've got real problems to worry about." I lowered my arms and propped one hand on my hip. "You've got five seconds to tell me what you want or I'm leaving."

"Oh, you think you've got a backbone?" Keira retorted. "Talking back to me like that."

I stepped around her, ignoring her approach and facing my father directly. "You had your assistant contact me. I'm in no mood for any games. Talk."

He frowned, not pleased about my strong arrival. "I summoned you on Tuesday!"

"*Summoned* me? I'm not a dog to call to heel." I was still confused about why he'd contacted me at all. He had to want something. That was the only reason he'd ever contact me. What he wanted, I had no clue. But just knowing he wanted something was a form of power I would wield with caution.

"You were supposed to be here Wednesday," he growled, impatient.

"Tough shit," I sassed back. "I couldn't get away."

"From what?" Keira mocked. "As if you have a life."

I narrowed my eyes at her but decided she couldn't be worthy of my energy. I had intended to come on Wednesday as he'd demanded. But then Mom had to be rushed to the hospital. Another infection. Then one of the horses got injured, and I had to beg the vet to come quickly even though I still owed him for the last two visits. Sheep got out. The shearing processor machine broke down. Then Oscar got into an accident with the better truck we used at the farm. As soon as I brought Mom home from the hospital, she fell into one of her depressive states, claiming that she was a burden on my soul.

Some days, it really felt like she was. And I hated to think that. Only when I was overly stressed did I let myself get down like that. I loved her. She was all I had, but when she was overwhelmed from her illness and hopelessness, my heart broke. I wore too many hats as it was, advocating for her health and running the farm, but when she needed comfort, I had to slow down even more and make sure she knew I could be present and that I loved her no matter what.

I was stretched too thin, dammit. So if my father and stepmother had any plans to waste my time, I would snap.

"I'm here now. Take it or leave it."

They exchanged a glance, seeming to communicate with just that look.

He rounded the desk, standing next to Keira.

"Sit," she instructed.

"No." I crossed my arms again. I was on edge, cautious and assuming this would be a trap. I wouldn't let them impose an air of power over me, looking down at me.

"That hardly matters," my father said, sighing.

"You said you would cover my mother's medical bills and debts. That you would see to covering her continued medical costs." That alone would be a massive weight off my shoulders. Maybe then, I could focus on making her farm less of a mediocre business and more a thriving one with an actual staff, new equipment, and more freedom to invest in it.

"And we will." She looked past me, smiling sweetly. "Oh, there you are, honey." Her voice dripped with sugar as Saoirse entered the room.

She passed me, knocking her bony shoulder against me, and I rolled my eyes.

"So, she finally showed up," Saoirse said, grinning as she dropped into a chair. Looking at me like she knew something I didn't, she crossed her legs and bounced her heeled foot.

I was getting sick of these jabs about being late. I couldn't stop and drop what I was doing to come here and play games.

"What's the catch?" I demanded, losing my patience.

"You get married to the man who wants *me*," Saoirse said as she looked up at her mother, beaming.

"What?" I deadpanned, wondering if this was a prank, if they were so bored that they had to call me to drive all the way out here as a joke.

"You marry the man interested in making Saoirse his bride. And in exchange, we will cover all of Nora's bills and expenses." Keira locked her malicious gaze on me, putting the ball in my court.

"Marry some guy? And you'll pay off her bills?" I asked, stunned.

My father nodded. "Tomorrow."

My jaw dropped. "You want me to marry someone tomorrow?"

"He is eager to find a bride," he added.

I narrowed my eyes. That was a hell of a big catch. "What's wrong with him?" Glancing at Saoirse and noticing how happy she was to be off the hook, I worried.

"Who cares?" Keira said. "Don't you want your mother's bills covered?"

"We've looked into your finances. Her farm and all that she owes." My father held his head higher. "You'll never get on top of it all to afford her kidney transplant."

Dammit. He really knew how to strike me down. Then again, Keira had a point. If all I had to do was marry some guy, so what? If it meant my mother would no longer suffer as much, if she wouldn't have those depressive spells about being in bed and so weak...

It would be worth it. I would do anything to improve her prognosis. Besides, if the guy was so terrible, I could divorce him later, right? They weren't saying that I had to *stay* married to him.

That's it. I hid the smile wanting to break across my face. A loophole. "You're saying that you'll pay for my mom's expenses if I show up at a wedding tomorrow and marry this guy?"

All three nodded.

I can't believe I'm going to do this...

But I would. I'd been drowning under the oppression of having no other options with the struggles of my life, but here was one dropped in my lap.

I thrust my hand out and held my breath, nervous but excited. "Fine."

My father looked at my hand, scrunching his nose in disgust.

"Shake on it," I demanded.

He did, his fingers weak and light around mine. "Tomorrow," he said.

I nodded, overwhelmed with all that I'd need to do. I had to call Oscar and tell him to go ahead and sell that tractor to hire help. That I wouldn't be back on the farm. Then, I bet I could ask old Mrs. Gehring across the road to come by and help my mother to and from her appointments. Oscar could step up and help her. I was glad I'd just picked up all of her prescriptions.

The butler took me to a guestroom in the basement, and I tuned out all the details that Keira told him. To get a dress fitted for me. To find someone to fix my hair and tend to my nails. If she was hoping for a makeover, she'd be disappointed. I refused to let them do anything but fit me for a gown while I tended to everything with Oscar over the phone.

"Will your mother be there?" he huffed, incredulous about this sudden news that I'd get married. "Can she travel for the wedding?"

"No." I shook my head, looking at my reflection in the mirror. I wished she would be at my wedding, but even if she could come, she'd be so upset to know I was bartering myself for her care. "I'll explain it to her later. Just tell her that a more lucrative work deal came through. Tell her whatever seems believable, not the truth."

I fell asleep in the strange room, unused to such a firm mattress, but my body was tired from the long day of work and the drive. My mind was weary from all the stress and now this new change.

Married. Tomorrow, I would be someone's wife.

When I opened my eyes, I got up with frayed nerves. I knew *nothing* about my groom, and I tried my best not to think about him at all on the drive to the church, then as I was led to the room in the back to get ready.

My father didn't want to walk me down the aisle. He explained that he'd be sitting with Keira to make sure I saw this through.

As if I wouldn't. I couldn't chance losing a free ticket to financial freedom and a better standing for my mother to get that kidney transplant. Marrying this man would solve all of my immediate problems.

So when I stepped out of the room to begin walking down the aisle, I lifted my face and started ahead with determination and shaky confidence.

I can do this. I will *do this, for Mom.*

I'd never thought about marrying. I'd only ever counted on a lifetime of working at the farm.

As I locked my gaze on the tall, brutish man scowling from the altar, I froze mid-step.

Oh, my God.

He looked like a thug. Hard and dangerous. Scarred and so stern, narrowing his eyes as he waited for me to continue down the aisle.

Him? I had to marry *him*? He looked like he'd just gotten out of jail. His black eye attested to violence, and with the way his muscled frame filled out his tux, he looked like a monster in fine clothing. A wolf in a sheep's hide.

"Oh, fuck," I whispered as I tried to will my feet to carry me forward.

That man instilled nothing but fear to make my heart race. His intense stare provoked me to tense up, my fight or flight instinct activated.

He looked like a heartless, impossible-to-please killer.

I didn't think. I couldn't comprehend how anyone could expect me to marry a rugged, lethal-looking man like that. I was so stunned and insulted, I couldn't remember my reasoning to go through with this.

My body reacted. I couldn't commit to being with someone who looked that scary.

And I turned to run away as fast as I could.

5

DECLAN

White lace and satin flowed after the redhead as she turned and fled. She gripped the skirt of her dress and sprinted down the aisle and away.

What the fuck?

Ian frowned at me, then turned toward Shane and Keira, like I did.

She fucking ran. After giving me a stern glare, she ran!

"What the hell is going on, Murray?" I stalked over to him, ready to punch his panicked face in.

"Cara!" Keira seethed, running after the redhead.

"Cara?" Ian was at my side.

"Who the fuck is Cara?" I demanded as I gripped the front of Murray's shirt.

"My, my, my daughter," Shane admitted, leaning back as I pulled him close.

I gritted my teeth. "Your daughter?" Right then, Saoirse entered the empty church from a side door. She wasn't wearing a white gown. She didn't look like a bride.

"What the fuck is going on? Are you trying to renege?" I shook him, straining with the urge to kill him.

"No!" He gripped my hands, trying to pull my fingers free. Stinking of nervous sweat, he panted and cringed at my tight hold on his shirt cinching at his neck.

"Where'd she go?" Saoirse whined, stomping her foot. "Daddy! You said she'd marry him because she's your oldest."

"Cara is my daughter," Shane said. "My first daughter. With Nora Gallagher. She was my girlfriend before I married Keira."

Keeping Shane right where he was, I turned to Ian. "Do you know anything about this?"

He shook his head, just as mad as I was.

"If you let me..." Shane fought to get free, reaching not to remove my hand from his shirt but to reach inside his jacket. "I worried you might not believe me. But I have..."

I released him, pushing him back with a shove. He staggered and held up a paper. After I snatched it and read it over, I gave it to Ian to see.

Cara Gallagher, daughter of Nora Gallagher and Shane Murray. The fucker had a backup daughter, and he expected me to marry her instead of the whiny bitch behind him.

Dad only needed me to marry someone from another reputable family. I wouldn't call Shane Murray anything but a spineless idiot, but he was from an Irish Mob Family. And his first daughter seemed to have more of a backbone than he did.

"I'm not going to marry *him*," Saoirse whined, pouting from the side of the empty pew.

I narrowed my eyes at her, wishing she'd shut up already. "No, you're fucking not." If I had a choice, I'd go for the redhead with vivid green eyes. A woman who'd try to stand up to me and go against orders. Someone with fire.

Keira rushed back into the church, out of breath and furious. She flapped her arm up and let it fall to her side. "I can't find her! She just took off and—' Scowling at her husband, she shook her head in warning. "*You* go chase her down and demand that she see this through. I will not let this monster marry Saoirse."

If this weren't my wedding day, I would've killed her for that insult. I was sick of her attitude, and I saw that her daughter would be a replica.

No. I wanted the woman who looked at me like she dared me to consider her my bride. It'd be entertaining, at least, to bend her to my will.

"Keep him there," I told Ian, pointing at the priest. "She couldn't have run far."

I strode out of the church, ignoring the heavy front doors and instead going toward the small courtyard toward the side. Keira must not have looked very hard, or Cara hid, because I found my future wife.

Her ass in the air. Her slender arms reaching up. Strong fingers gripping bricks on the wall.

"Going somewhere?" I growled as she tried to escape.

She turned her head, not stopping her climb, and glowered at me. "Leave me alone."

Not a chance in hell I'll do that.

I stalked closer, admiring her curvy yet toned body. She wasn't frumpy with fat, nor was she skinny with no substance. Graceful and athletic.

"Get down."

"I don't take orders from you."

I gritted my teeth, annoyed and excited that she'd be so dumb as to push back. "Think again, *wife*."

"I'm *not* your wife." She growled, trying to reach for a higher rock. "And I won't be your anything—" She fell, dropping into my arms. I held her soft weight snugly in my arms, but she was wild to be free of me. Her elbow jabbed into my neck, and with the many layers of her billowing dress, the satiny fabric made her too slippery to hold on to.

She broke away, backing to the stone wall. Limping but not caving to any injury she might have gotten from that fall, she glared at me, unafraid to look me in the eye with that heated sass. Huffing a breath up to clear her red hair from her face, she backpedaled until I had her cornered against the wall.

Up close, she was gorgeous. Mad and riled up. Her freckled cheeks blushed while her parted lips let in shallow inhales. Her tits practically spilled out of her dress, plump and begging for my touch. But that gaze, so furious and determined…

Fuck, she was something else.

"You're going to be my wife," I said. "I'll fuck you right here against this wall and force the union on you through consummation."

She rolled her eyes. "Don't tell me my stepsister doesn't appeal more."

She doesn't even compare.

"*You* will be my wife."

"No."

I tilted my head to the side. "You will be my wife long enough so you can give me an heir."

Her brow furrowed. "What?"

"All I need is a goddamn heir. Nothing more. I don't give a shit who my wife is so long as I get an heir."

She licked her lips, taunting me to taste her mouth right here. To nip at her and make her hiss. Anything. Everything. I was two seconds from ramming into her right here in this courtyard.

Her phone pinged, and she glanced down at it, still tense with confusion. When she blinked quickly, she shook her head and mumbled something to herself, something so low that I couldn't understand.

"What?"

"I..." She met my gaze again, troubled yet calculating. "You need an heir?"

"That's what I fucking said."

Her throat tensed and flexed as she struggled to swallow. Pale and seeming more scared, she lifted her chin defiantly.

Goddamn, she was ballsy. She had gumption, facing me like this. If she could put up a fight like this, not too timid and frightened to give me all she got, it would be all too easy to slam into her cunt and overpower her. To conquer her. To claim and possess her.

"I'll marry you under one condition."

I laughed once. How cute. She thought she had any grounds to negotiate with me? I realized that Shane couldn't have been honest with her about *why* she had to marry me, and I was slightly intrigued about what motivated her to show up at all to a wedding when she had no clue who her groom was.

"A condition?"

She scowled at my mocking tone. "What's your name?" she demanded.

So, she was told nothing? It didn't matter. "Declan Sullivan."

Arching one brow, she reacted as though she'd never heard of me before. It wasn't hard to see how Shane—and Keira—had likely cast her and Nora aside. The man hadn't ever acknowledged a second daughter. Her ignorance about who I was made sense.

"I will marry you on one condition."

I crossed my arms, curious. "Go on," I goaded her without any intention to agree to her criteria. I was in charge here. I was the boss. Not her.

"If I'm not pregnant within… six months, I can leave you."

Leave? She would marry me if she had a way out?

I stared at her, trying to understand how she'd come to that conclusion. She really didn't know much about the Mob ways of life. Couples didn't split and get divorced. That was too trivial, a waste of time. When you married, you married for life. To the death.

The idea of my third wife not sticking around forever was a joke. She would be mine until she died. But it wasn't up to me to educate her about that fact now.

"Six months?" I asked, pretending to consider it.

"Yes. If I don't give you an heir, then I can leave." She nodded once, as if repeating her scheme made more sense the second time she heard it out loud.

Fuck no.

I extended my hand for her to shake it. "It's a deal," I lied.

She narrowed her eyes, cautious as she stepped forward. Her fingers hovered over mine until she lowered her hand and touched me. The first press of her warm grip surprised me. Firm, strong. She was no weakling, bold and not too shy to give me a real shake.

"Deal," she agreed, stepping closer.

I kept my hand on hers, tugging her out from the pebbles lining the path, and hauled her right back into the church.

I hadn't realized how fun this would end up being.

At her attempts to pull her hand from mine, I grinned, knowing she would never run away from me again.

You're mine. For good. Whether you like it or not.

6

CARA

Declan didn't let me go. Each time I tried to wrench my hand free, his fingers locked down tighter. If it wasn't a show of his strength, a reminder that he was bigger and stronger, it was a sign of how badly he wanted this wedding to happen.

I didn't need another example of his power. He'd caught me—easily and without so much as a grunt of exertion—when I fell from the wall I'd so foolishly thought I could climb over. Really, in heels and this enormous dress with so many layers I felt like I was wrapped in a bubble of lace? It had been a dumb plan to try to run. The front doors were locked, which raised red flags.

The courtyard had no exits, and a knee-jerk reaction to the vision of having to be with Declan for the rest of my life had me panicking and wishing to run.

He frightened me, even if he was strong and able to prevent me from crashing to the path and breaking a bone. It still hurt. I'd sprained my ankle, and it throbbed as he hurried me back into the empty church.

I didn't say anything. I didn't utter a damn word, and I refused to let out a sound of discomfort or pain. Letting this man see me vulnerable would be too much to bear. With someone so dark and impatient as him, I had to make sure I presented myself as an equal, not a thing to push around.

Even if he literally dragged me like I was an object to place at the altar.

I didn't bother smiling, facing him off with all the disdain and irritation I could muster. He didn't care. Staring right back with that frustrated glare, he gave me the impression that making him run after me was a grievance he didn't care for.

Why? Why me?

As the timid priest cleared his throat and began speaking, Declan squeezed my hand tighter. A signal that this was happening.

But why?

Tiring of maintaining this glower on Declan, I shifted my focus to the only other people in the room.

Shane and Keira stood together in the first pew. They'd switched sides, standing behind Declan, and I couldn't look away.

My father had never acknowledged me. Not once in my life once he met Keira. I thought back to how he'd been so annoyed with my late arrival to his mansion, disobeying his request that I come speak to him about that "favor" earlier this week.

Behind him, Saoirse smirked. Smug and stuck up. I seldom ever spoke to her, but it all clicked now without any words needing to be shared.

Declan must have made an offer for *her*. And seeing what a hulking thug Declan was, she'd refused.

That's why. My father expected me to marry Declan so Saoirse wouldn't have to. I was the backup. The sacrifice. The spare to dispose of.

Keira tipped her chin higher, and I was pulled to consider her haughty expression as the priest droned on. She slit her eyes, honing her anger on me.

You fucking bitch. I didn't react to her direct glower. I kept my face masked and locked in this frown as I revisited the image of my phone. I'd received a text from her when I'd so idiotically tried to escape in the church's courtyard.

Keira texted me a simple warning, *Marry that man or else.* Attached was a picture taken of a document. I'd stared at that simple paper many times, wondering if and when my mother would be not only accepted for the kidney transplant, but also to be matched before it was too late.

I didn't want to know how Keira got her hands on a copy of that document from the farm. She knew how to use it with maximum effectiveness.

Marry him or your mother will be taken off the waitlist for this.

Her text chilled me. And just like that, I caved to her threat. I couldn't forsake my mother. I couldn't compromise her hope for a healthier rest of her life. My cooperation in all of this was contingent on that detail. That was the only way I could go through with this wedding, nodding and mumbling my replies to the priest.

Only for her.

She was the only reason that made this bearable.

Declan tugged on my hand, noticing that I looked around. If he worried I was trying to run again, he could relax on that. His ironclad grip on my hand was no joke. My fingers would go numb soon, but still, I refused to show him that he was hurting me.

Do your worst, asshole. Go on. I dare you. Because I would be the winner here.

Little did he know, but I couldn't carry a child. I had very limited chances of fertility due to complications with an ovarian cyst rupture when I first entered puberty. Scar tissue had rendered me damaged and unlikely to ever conceive, so the joke was on him.

My idea to strike a deal with him was an impulsive decision. I knew I was marrying him to secure my mother's health and safety, but I couldn't just leave her or my home. I had to get back to her. Once my father paid her bills, I'd be nearly free to return to her.

I wouldn't give Declan an heir.

I would let him consider me his wife for mere months. Then I would be the one walking away victorious. I'd be the one to get what I wanted, and I couldn't trouble myself with feeling a morsel of guilt about it.

He was only using me. He only wanted me to knock me up. He'd told me so bluntly that he didn't care who his wife was, just as long as he had one and she could give him a child. His frankness peeved me, proving how much he didn't give a shit about me.

Of course, he doesn't care. He's not in this for love or money or anything else. A man who'd enter an arranged marriage—and force it upon his bride—wouldn't even consider the normal reasons a couple would be united.

I hadn't ever thought about marrying. Independence mattered too much, and once I toughed out these six months, I would actually, finally, have some taste of it. Without my mother's medical woes and debts weighing down on me...

"Ow." I hissed, losing my stride with not showing Declan any discomfort. He'd squeezed harder on my hand, and I furrowed my brow at him.

The priest cleared his throat, ripping my attention from the jerk who'd be my husband.

"What?" I snapped.

Blushing and timidly glancing at Declan, the priest gestured at a hand reaching out to me.

Another man seemed to bite his lip, struggling not to laugh as he held up a ring for me to take from him.

I'd zoned out so much, I wasn't paying attention to the ceremony.

I made eye contact with the tuxedoed man and took the ring.

"Got yourself a really sweet one here, Dec," he teased.

"Shut the fuck up, Ian." Declan held his hand up for me to slip his ring on. I did, ramming it over his knuckle and pushing it hard enough to sting as it hit his palm.

"You sure she's going to stick around?" Ian whispered back with too much amusement.

"Shut up," I told Ian, annoyed. I didn't need any more damn reminders of my stupidity to escape the first time. I wouldn't lose sight of what mattered. My mother was dependent on my obedience here, and I wouldn't risk her life.

Declan took the simple band and positioned it to slide up my finger. I expected him to force it onto my digit like I had done to him. I knew nothing at all about this man, but I counted on a devilish malice with how cruelly and wickedly he glared at me.

Instead of pain, I was teased to a slow drag of the cool metal up my finger. He pressed it up until it rested as far as it could go. Then, keeping his crystal blue eyes on me, he raised my hand to his smirking lips to kiss where the jewelry now resided.

Heat flared through me, confusing me and pissing me off. The touch of his mouth on me should've repulsed me, but my body wasn't on the same page as my mind. It was the sinister promise in his stare that ignited this ridiculous spike of lust.

"She won't be going anywhere," he vowed in reply to his best man.

I swallowed, narrowing my eyes at what sounded like a threat to fight against.

But it also seemed to be a genuine oath, that he would ensure that I stay captive as his bride.

"Six months," I reminded him in a hot whisper.

His lips lifted in a cruel smile, and I bit my lip not to shout at him.

"If you dare to renege…"

He spoke over my heated whisper, answering the priest with an *I do*.

"I'll run," I warned, stepping closer to whisper. "I'll run so fucking fast if you back out of our agreement."

The priest cleared his throat again, and without acknowledging him, I maintained this glare on my groom and through clenched teeth, replied, "I do."

Declan didn't waste a second. His hand left mine at last. Reaching up to grip the back of my neck, he hauled me close for a punishing kiss. His lips dominated, forcing me back without any room to move as he locked his hand on me, securing my head right where he wanted me.

Fuck.

I was overwhelmed, stunned and shocked. He claimed my mouth, infusing heat and angry passion against my lips with a brutal urgency I couldn't deny. Desire tricked me into wanting to moan and reply in kind. Fear kept me nervous and bewildered.

A potent burst of lust spiraled within me, but the stubborn insistence to appear unaffected and unchanging won out.

I froze, doing my best to ignore how fucking good his lips were against mine. Warm, firm, and so ravenous.

He broke away, staring at me with mere inches buffering between us.

Those blue orbs glittered with desire and power, maybe a hint of mischief too, as though he was laughing at me.

Fuck you. I'd be damned if he'd mock me, if he thought he could get under my skin in any way at all.

Narrowing my eyes, I waited for him to release the back of my neck. Deep down, I resisted the pull to him, to grab his jacket and tug him back down so I could have a repeat of that hot kiss, to ask for a longer dose of that desire I had no business feeling for *him*.

Tough it out, then run. That's all I have to do.

"You're mine now, Cara," he growled.

Not for good.

Ian chuckled. "Shall we leave for the reception?"

I flinched, jarred by the realization that it wasn't just me and Declan here. That we weren't in this bubble of desire and anger, antagonizing each other in private.

The priest had scurried away. My "family" filed to the exit.

Ian waited for Declan and me to leave.

"Reception?" I asked, dodging his grip.

"Yes." He smoothed down his jacket. "An evil necessity we must endure to make this look as believable as possible."

You *are my evil necessity.* I held up my hand, showing him the band he'd placed on my finger. "This is proof enough."

He grabbed my hand and held it, leading me down the aisle. "My family will need to meet you."

I rolled my eyes. "But they couldn't bother to come to the ceremony?"

"The ceremony you tried to flee?"

I rolled my eyes, looking aside and trying to brace myself for a party to meet his family and the people whose opinions he cared about.

My family wasn't here. My mother was home, likely confused about why I'd taken off. Struck with a deep sense of homesickness, I followed my husband out of the church and tried to convince myself that I could handle this.

That I could handle anything he dared to throw at me.

Just so long as he doesn't try to weaken me by kissing me ever again.

7

DECLAN

Cara stayed at my side all through the reception.

It seemed like a waste of time and energy to throw a party celebrating my third wedding.

The first one with Erin was the fanciest, with five hundred guests. It ended with two separate brawls and three men killed.

Marrying Caitlin resulted in more drama, even though the guest list was smaller and the evening was short and simple.

This time, only a couple of hundred partiers drank and mingled in the grand reception hall Ian had secured when Shane complained that he wasn't having luck finding anything in his "budget".

Celebrating in a crowd wasn't my preference, and there wasn't any victory here. I'd put my ring on yet another bride. The real test that I cared about was whether she'd live long enough to bear my child.

Which is all the more reason to fucking go now.

Ian caught my attention at the head table, raising his brows as if he'd heard my thoughts.

I had no interest in pretending to be a newlywed with Cara. The faster I got her alone and fucked her, my true purpose with her would be settled. For tonight, at least. I'd soak her cunt with my cum until it took root and she was pregnant.

That was all I needed from her.

Yet, as I turned and glanced at her again, hearing her sigh once more, I felt stuck with this nagging curiosity to want to know more about her.

She was a stranger, one reluctantly connected to me forever.

And I knew not a single thing about the gorgeous redhead.

Other than the fact that she's far from happy about being here. I could give credit where it was due. Every time guests came up to congratulate her, she faked a polite smile and pretended to be engaged with small talk. It was all a lie. She was just as sick as I was of sitting around here while this party dragged on.

It proved how little she would care about her marriage with me, and I wondered what she did value. What she cared about.

What made you change your mind?

I respected her bravery. Cara didn't pout or stomp like a petulant child about marrying me like her stepsister had. No. Cara ran, trying to take charge of her life and do what she wanted. She'd taken a risk in attempting to flee as soon as she saw me. It didn't bother me that the mere sight of me had frightened her off.

She couldn't have been scared because of my reputation. While we stood at the altar, I wondered if she'd balked because she'd heard about the misfortunes that found my previous wives. My track record wasn't stellar, but she hadn't even known my name.

It hardly mattered what intimidated her about me. She'd stood there, bold and pissed, and said her *I do*.

But why?

I glanced at Shane across the hall. He sat with Keira as the woman ranted at him.

What a life. I wouldn't be a husband to be nagged by my wife. I didn't plan on being near her long enough to hold a conversation with her. Just to fuck her. That was all I needed.

Shane had to have held something over her to get her to comply. Something he'd used as leverage to get his unacknowledged and cast-aside eldest daughter to coerce her to marry me.

I wonder what that text was.

As soon as Cara's phone pinged, she'd been reminded of why she should go along with this marriage. Her face had paled. She'd looked terrified. Whatever that message was, it convinced her to become the next Mrs. Sullivan.

She sipped her water, meeting my gaze, and I wanted to kiss her fucking smirk off her lips.

Yeah, hate me all you want. I'm not having fun either.

"Dec."

I turned the other way, facing Ian. He tipped his chin toward the other side of the dance floor. Cara and I hadn't bothered. Dancing was for fools. Just like the two men walking among the guests out there.

Peter Boyle and the same asshole who'd accused one of my fighters of cheating.

"How the fuck did they get in here?" I demanded.

Ian shrugged, moving to stand.

"No. I'll deal with them." I held my hand out to him, suggesting that he stand guard over Cara. She'd stuck at my side the whole two hours we were here. I didn't trust her not to leave. She was already showing as a flight risk.

By the time I crossed the dance floor, they were dealt with. Another man I trusted had reached them and gotten them to think twice about coming here to spy or otherwise stir up trouble. Many members of the crime families were here. Some as allies, others as enemies, and more as something in between. But the Boyles were by far my father's nemesis, and I refused to let them stay.

When I turned back to the table, surprised with how badly I wanted to be near my sexy wife again, I stopped short.

She wasn't there.

The table was empty.

Fuck!

I hurried toward Ian, who spoke with a dignitary who liked having our protection. He smiled, mingling and doing that diplomatic, bureaucratic bullshit I didn't have the patience for. As soon as he noticed me storming close, he frowned.

"What's wrong?" He leaned to look past me. "Is Boyle—"

I grabbed the front of his jacket and pulled him closer, yanking him out of his conversation. "Where is she?"

He huffed. "On the patio outside. She wanted a breath of fresh air."

Ignoring how he looked at me like I was insane to be this worried, I released him and glowered at the floor-to-ceiling windows that showed the darkness of the night out there.

"Dec." He smoothed down his jacket where I'd wrinkled the garment. "Relax. The guards are out there."

"She's a runner. I can tell." I wouldn't update him about how she'd tried to make a deal with me to let her go in six months. I had no intention to ever give her up. Besides, couldn't he understand how dire this was? Cara had to work out. She had to give me an heir. Dad wouldn't live long enough for Ian to locate another bride for me.

"You're seriously going to hover over her?" He shook his head, amused. "Relax," he repeated. "The guards would stop her from running."

I didn't believe him. I jogged outside, seeking her in the shadows. When I didn't spot her immediately, my heart raced. Adrenaline filled me. I wanted a fight. I was spoiling for one, eager to vent this instant anger that she'd fucking run off.

"Fuck!" I grumbled to myself as I stalked around, searching through the gardens out back. The landscaped area offered numerous paths leading to fountains and artistic hedges. It would be too easy for someone to sneak away with this confusing labyrinth of greenery. And she was determined, too.

"You fucking little—"

I stopped short, losing the other half of my complaint as I found her.

Seated on a granite bench, she rolled her head like she was erasing the kinks in her tight neck.

Clamping my lips shut, I gritted my teeth and stalked toward her. "What the fuck do you think you're doing?"

She whirled around, standing as she pivoted on the bench. "What?" Narrowing her eyes, she lost that slight peaceful expression she wanted to hide from me.

"What the fuck are you doing?" I grabbed her arm, bringing her with me out of this clearing of soft grass. She wobbled in her heels, struggling to walk as quickly as I did over the lawn.

"I was getting a breath of fresh air!" She struggled to wrench free, and I growled, turned on and riled up even more by her antagonism.

"The fuck you were." I leaned back, hoisting her up and over my shoulder.

"Declan! Put me down!"

"You were going to run." I gritted my teeth as she wriggled to get free.

"I wasn't. Goddammit! I just wanted fresh air!"

She wiggled and fought, shouting obscenities at me as I hastened to carry her straight to one of the cars waiting on the drive.

Putting her down wasn't possible. The longer I kept her in my arms, touching her with my hands, I *knew* she was here. With me. Without anywhere to go. The relief of finding her and catching her was bliss, but just entertaining the possibility that my third wife could have left me too soon had me furious.

I shoved her, fighting and growling, into the backseat. Then I exhaled hard, my nostrils flaring, as I rounded the car to get in the driver's seat. The uniformed valet worker trembled, mouth open in fear and shock, as I held out my hand.

"Give me the fucking key."

He did, and I wasted no time speeding out of there and taking Cara straight to my house. Tuning out her threats and shouts, I focused on getting her to my bed as quickly as possible. Driving to the estate house in the country would take too long. I couldn't manage that much of a wait. I had to take her. *Now*. I had to show her in the simplest yet complicated way that she was fucking mine no matter how much she'd try to run.

"I just wanted to *breathe*!" she snapped, wrestling with the billowy layers of her dress. She was surrounded by the material in the backseat, frustrated and batting down the material.

Oh, I'll get you out of that shit in just a fucking minute.

I parked, slamming on the brakes hard enough that she jolted forward. She put her hand up to stop the impact against the back of my seat, but by the time I got out and wrenched open the back door, she'd scrambled back to the other side of the car.

I wasn't fast enough. She was still so determined. At any other time, in any other circumstances, I would've admired that she didn't give up.

I ran around the car as she stood. Holding her hands out, warding me off, she caught her breath. "Stop!"

"Don't tell me what to do."

"You don't have to haul me around!" She glanced at the mansion and grunted. "I can walk."

You sassy woman. Desire swelled within me as I passed her, taking her hand and pulling her inside.

I never cared to have much staff here, and I made sure no one would be on duty tonight. I wanted all the freedom to stuff my dick into Cara's pussy as much as I wanted without any interruption. If I were lucky, she'd carry my child from tonight's efforts alone and spare me the obligation to try again.

Slamming her against the back of the door after I closed it, though, I realized it wouldn't be a chore at all.

Her fiery glare made my blood burn hotter. The sight of her tits damn near spilling out taunted me. And the stubborn lift of her chin challenged me.

"Bend over," I growled.

She grunted in surprise as I whirled her around fast. Her hands shot out, slamming against the old wood panel.

I yanked at her dress, shoving it up until I found her panties. One tug ripped them, but she protested.

"Declan. Can't—"

I grabbed her hands and smacked them to the door. "Keep your fucking hands right there."

I unzipped my pants and freed my cock, stiff as steel and dripping moisture. She was temptation personified, making me ache for her submission. And I didn't wait to claim it, to take her and possess her.

Keeping her dress up, I grabbed her hips and tugged her back. She gasped at the first touch. I lined my dick up with her slit, but I paused.

Looking down at her pussy lips, her legs splayed wide from my kicks at her feet to open up her stance, I watched the glistening smear of her cream as I held my cockhead right there.

She was wet.

She was…

She wanted it. She wanted me. Even though she'd protested, she was aroused.

So I notched myself deeper, watching my mushroomed head disappear into her pink flesh.

She arched back, and I grabbed both of her hands in one of mine. Shoving her hands back to the door, I followed through and thrust my dick into her.

Every hard inch. All the way into her tight, slick pussy. She choked me, squeezing me in so hard that I growled at the intensity of pressure.

She either hadn't done this in a while or—

A virgin.

Fuck. I hadn't counted on that. I should have. She had to be at least fifteen years younger than me, but I hadn't anticipated this gift.

"Fuck."

She cried out, sobbing instantly at the intrusion.

I didn't stop. It felt too fucking good. Like heaven. A rare treasure. I hammered her cunt, pulling out and driving back in so fast that her head hung low until she hit it against the door.

Soon, her cries turned to gasps. And with every torturous glide back and forth as I stretched her, I felt the tension of her inner walls clamping down on me. Slick with her juices, I stared as my dick sank into her over and over. Until my balls tightened. My spine zinged with pressure. And I came.

I continued fucking her as hard as I could, flooding her womb with my hot cum. Jerking from the force of losing my load in her, I punched my hips toward hers.

Her pussy fluttered, still reacting with waves of her own orgasm as I pinned her to the door. Exhausted from the burn and buildup of wanting to fuck her, I leaned against the entrance until my knees weren't as shaky, until I could straighten and pull out of her tight sheath.

She winced, her head turned sideways and pressed against the door. Her eyes remained closed, and I watched as my cum dribbled down her thighs.

I reached over and flicked the lock on the door she rested upon. The sound jarred her, and she opened her eyes.

Without stepping back, I reached low to thrust two of my fingers into her, shoving my cum back inside.

"Don't even think about running," I warned.

Then I turned, heading to bed without another glance at the thoroughly fucked woman who was no longer a virgin.

My wife.

8

CARA

When I woke up to my first day as a married woman, the first thing I noticed was the complete, utter silence. It cloaked me, pressing me down into the bed I'd found in one of the many guest rooms here.

Declan left me at the door, and this was the first room I found that seemed prepared for a guest.

Guest? I was no guest. For the next six months, I would be a resident here.

This wasn't anything like being at home, at the only residence I knew at Mom's farm.

No sounds of animals woke me up. No urgency filled me with the rush to feed the sheep and horses. Not a single beep nor chirp of the birds and other wildlife out in the open land.

It was… unsettling. Like I was the last person alive on Earth.

As I opened my eyes and took stock of the tenderness between my legs, I realized that meant this foreign pain signified that my mother would be one day closer to getting her life-changing surgery. In exchange for losing my virginity and marrying Declan, she was that much nearer the chance to have a semi-normal life.

He raped me. Thinking it felt like a crime, but I had to succumb to accepting it as my new reality. I was married. And my husband had raped me.

I blinked, zoning out at the ceiling as the tenderness lingered with a dull throb.

Declan had raped me. He'd accused me of trying to run away right after our damn wedding, and he took his anger out by slamming into me so hard, and holding on to my hips with such a forceful grip, that bruises would no doubt line my skin for days.

I lay there, rubbing my eyes and waiting for a reason to get up.

This should have felt like a vacation. A blessing. A stroke of luck. Waking up with zero obligations like what welcomed me at the farm should've felt like a break that I never imagined I could have in life.

It didn't.

Recalling how forcefully Declan had overpowered me at the door scared me. His gruff treatment bewildered me, and until I could figure out how to acclimate to him, I wasn't sure how to behave, what to do, and how I would stay sane for the next six months.

I'd never had sex before. At the farm, I lacked the time to make friends, socialize, date, or get to the point that I could sleep with someone. From dawn to dusk, I worked my ass off and tried to multi-task to handle *everything* for my mom.

That didn't mean I hadn't thought of how I might lose it. The brutal possession Declan had done last night wasn't it.

"Does it matter, though?" I whispered aloud, still waiting for something to propel me to get up.

It couldn't matter. Eventually, I would've probably tried to spend a little more time to figure out how to pleasure myself in the privacy of my own room. Just to take the edge off and seek release. That was only a human need, anyway.

Not once did I ever plan to marry, to have a family. I couldn't get pregnant, and I'd come to terms with that a long time ago. All I ever had was my mother, and after she was gone, I knew that I wouldn't want to be a burden for anyone else but myself.

"Good luck with that." I rolled my eyes as I sat up and winced at the soreness down there. Sitting was worse, and I shifted to stand and ease the pressure on my ass where he'd slammed into me with his hips.

For the next five months and twenty-nine days, I would be with Declan, and already, I felt like the biggest burden to the grumpy asshole. He was so nervous about my running. I got it. I *did* run when I first saw him. That first impression wasn't helping my situation, but last night, I was sitting on a damn bench, not running. If he was going to be a caveman and haul me over his shoulder everywhere, or lock his fingers around my arm, I would scream.

I got it. He thought I was his. But did that have to mean hovering and supervising my every move? Treating me like a prisoner?

I narrowed my eyes at the reflection in the mirror, angry at the possibility that he'd plan to do just that.

He's not hovering now. I didn't know where he was in this huge house, and I really didn't care. Last night, I showered in this guest room, and once I found some women's clothing in the drawers—surprised to find both his and hers sets of garments—I hid away.

Distance helped. Because without his dark, molten gaze on me, it was far, far easier to forget about how good it felt when he pushed me to come.

"Let's just forget about that," I quipped quietly to myself.

Something had to be wrong with me to be turned on by that brute taking me so hard, and the less I thought about it, the calmer I would feel about this situation.

I doubted I'd be able to avoid him all day, though, so with all the courage and confidence I could gather without caffeine to fuel me, I opened the door and entered the hallway.

The whole house was quiet. No one stirred. I didn't detect a single sound of activity anywhere, but it didn't prompt me to call out for Declan. Or a staff member. He had to have one here, because like my father's home, only bigger, my husband resided in an enormous mansion. He sure wasn't the one dusting and sweeping around here, and everything looked immaculate.

It was a lot like being the only guest in a museum.

Quiet. Still. So many pieces of artwork and finely crafted furniture.

And locked in.

A lot like a prison, too.

I drew a deep breath and walked down the hall, peeking through open doorways, curious what else would be revealed here in the light of the day.

My exploration was cut short.

Two guards rounded the hallway and ran after me.

"Hey! Stop!"

I flinched, startled, and did the opposite. Seeing two humongous men chasing me down incited fear, and I turned and ran down the plush rug. Tall and fit, they reached me in no time. Their hands gripped my arms. One shackled his arm around my waist, and as he lifted me into the air, I kicked and thrashed.

"What the hell are you doing? Put me down. Let me go!" My orders fell on deaf ears, and they teamed up to contain me like I was a wild animal about to run.

First Declan and his highhandedness. Now these guards. What the hell kind of life did I marry into? I knew my father was affiliated with a crime family. I suspected that was why my mother had never reached out to him. Even if she wasn't too proud to go back to him after I was born, she was smart enough to avoid being tied to a Mob man. Here I'd gone and married one. Declan was so clearly a Mob leader. I didn't expect a peaceful existence as his wife, but was I even that? Or a prisoner?

The pair of guards didn't let me go, not once. Together, they tried to force me toward the door where Declan had raped me last night.

Anger trumped the fear searing through my veins. I was livid, exhausted and fed up with this rough manhandling. I could walk. Why couldn't they fucking tell me what to do, where I could go, and let me walk like a normal person?

"We need to get her to the estate," one said to the other, grunting as he fended off my kicks.

"She's not cooperating, though, is she?" the other snapped back.

"Then sedate her." The first one gripped my arm and wrenched it back, preparing to jam a needle into me.

"Stop!" My throat was hoarse from screaming, but I refused to let them treat me like a prisoner like this. I would protest and fight back until my last goddamn breath. They would win. They were bigger and stronger, armed with muscles and drugs. But I refused to make it easy for them.

"What the fuck is going on?"

The two men went still at Declan's bellow. They didn't release me, holding me tight as I still wrestled to get free. My husband's loud footsteps sounded down the hall as he rushed up to us, and I slowed my efforts to escape. Panting and furious, I stared up at him.

"She was trying to run," the second guard said.

"I was *not*," I shot back.

The guard narrowed his eyes, clenching his jaw like I'd pissed him off by arguing back.

"You surprised me." I exhaled long and hard, weary and tense. "You ran after me, and I reacted in fear."

"She ran from us, sir," the first man said. "We were attempting to transport her to the estate as you've requested, but she's straining to get away."

Declan furrowed his brow, noticing the syringe in the man's hand. He knocked it to the floor, gripping the front of the man's shirt.

"Are you fucking stupid? Drugging her?"

The guard nodded. "A sedative. Just to transport—"

"No drugs." He punched him hard. "She's my wife. She could be carrying my fucking heir."

I stayed quiet, biting my cheek. *Actually, no, I'm not.* He had no clue I would fail him with that task.

Once he finished punching the guard and warning him not to drug me—ever—he turned to me. His chest heaved. His eyes burned with impatience and annoyance.

"You'd better behave." He pointed at me, and the second guard released me. I rubbed my arm, glaring at my husband.

"You'd better fucking behave, or I'll teach you another lesson about what happens if you try to run from me."

Of course, he'd assume that I was putting up such a fuss because I wanted to run. I doubted there was anything I could do, anything I could even say to persuade him that I wouldn't escape until our deal was done.

Six months, asshole. Then I will run.

Instead of finding anything to tell him, any placating agreement to lower his rabid obsession about keeping me under his control, I settled for nothing at all.

Glowering at him, I tipped my chin up and relied on silence, loathing him with every fiber of my being.

No matter how good he'd felt when he forced that orgasm out of me last night.

9

DECLAN

Cara didn't say a word. She didn't run, either. With the way I found her in the hallway, held up by the guards who were tasked as her personal security, I wondered who to believe, whether they'd caught her trying to escape again, or she'd been startled.

But drugging her? No. Fuck no. I wouldn't risk anything complicating the health of my potential child. I'd only fucked her once last night, but even that could be enough. All it took was once.

After I showered and went to my bedroom, I failed to sleep. Intending to sample her sweet, tight pussy again, I found her in the guest room and debated taking her again.

But I didn't. I wasn't above fucking her while she was unconscious, but something held me back.

She liked it.

Even though she protested and fought me, I saw and felt the evidence of her arousal.

And that intrigued me. I'd only ever met hardcore whores and escorts who could take it rough and get off like that. Half the time, I suspected that they were faking it just to please me. But Cara hadn't. She'd dripped for me. She'd clenched around my dick so tightly as she came.

I wanted to take her harder next time, but when I could see how much she wanted. How far she could go in the realm of pain to seek her pleasure.

The whole ride to the family estate, she stared mulishly out the window, refusing to face me at all.

I didn't care. I hadn't married her for her company. The idea of a conversation intrigued me, but I bet she gave me the silent treatment to piss me off. Or maybe not. I simply didn't care. Talk or not. Be happy or not. All that mattered was her ability to give me a son or daughter.

When we arrived, I arranged for another pair of guards to take over her security. It wasn't only to keep her safe, because as my wife, she would have *my* enemies by association and would inherently be at risk. She also required a protection detail because she could escape.

No one could understand how important this was. My hopes of giving my father an heir before his death relied on her.

Once she was taken to her wing, an ornately decorated area that was decidedly feminine and would provide all she might want or need, I headed to check on my father.

After his death, this would be my home. It would be my residence to share with Cara and our children. I wouldn't give up my preferred residence, the mansion where I'd taken Cara last night. It would become more of a vacation home. But it made sense for her to adjust to living here.

For good.

Dad was awake and slightly agitated when I entered his room. Ian sat in the chair next to his bed. Upon my entrance, he nodded once and then sighed.

"You married her?" Dad asked. "You married…" He glanced at Ian as though to confirm the name again.

"Not Saoirse," Ian replied.

"Cara Gallagher," I said.

Dad shook his head, grimacing as he tried to sit up more. "I thought I told you to marry the other one. Saoirse."

"She wasn't interested."

"The hell with what *she* wanted," Dad thundered.

"Easy, easy," Ian warned carefully as Dad fell into a fitful coughing spell.

"And *I* wasn't interested," I added. One look at Saoirse and I wasn't intrigued. Not that it mattered whether I was. But the first glance at Cara's stubborn glare, and I knew she was the one I'd take home. "While it was news to me that Murray had an estranged daughter, she fit the bill."

And the fucker had some kind of leverage to force her to go along with the wedding.

"I showed him the birth certificate copy." Ian pointed at it on the side table.

"And I fear you've only found cause for a war," Dad muttered.

"What?" I narrowed my eyes, trying to figure out what he meant by that.

"Nora Gallagher." Dad picked up the certificate and furrowed his brow. "Supposedly a 'nobody'."

Ian nodded. "From what I've seen, she is no one special."

I believed him. Shane Murray had surprised us both yesterday with this secret daughter being revealed in the nick of time. And I had no doubt that Ian had researched Cara and her legitimacy as Shane's daughter right away. He was the office man. He handled those sorts of affairs. The guy had probably stayed up late looking into Cara's family history.

"Perhaps not," Dad grumbled, frowning at me. "Nora might be an illegitimate daughter of a member from the Boyle Family."

You've got to be fucking kidding me. "A Boyle?" *Cara is a distant relation of our biggest enemy?*

"I'm looking into it," Ian said. "It seems like it was just a rumor that Dad is relying on here."

"But," Dad argued, "if she is in any way related to the Boyles, and they find out that you have married into their line, they will see it as a grave transgression."

The Sullivans and Boyles have always fought. Sometimes literally. We always avoided a full-out war, but nothing was ever peaceful between us.

If they learned that I'd married into their family in any way, taking even a distant relative in marriage, this might cause a brutal battle.

"Do you think that's why Peter showed up with his guy last night?" I asked Ian. It had peeved me, seeing them among my guests at the reception, but I hadn't considered why they'd happened to stop by.

"I don't know." He shrugged, but didn't seem too worried. "I got the impression they were being nosy and happened to be around."

That was what I'd thought too. Until this news about Nora being an illegitimate daughter within their protection. Sons ruled. The patriarchy was strong within our families, but *every* child mattered. No one could cross loyalties, even by taking a wife associated with an enemy.

"This is bullshit." I fumed, looking from Dad's worried and tired eyes to Ian's sharp and alert ones. Fury coursed through me, heating me up and making my heart race faster with the need to fight.

I felt duped, like Murray had pulled the wool over my eyes. And that wouldn't do.

"Fucking Murray." I shook my head, gesturing for Ian to stand and come with me.

"I'll look into this," I promised my father. It was too late to renege. I'd married Cara. I'd consummated it too. She *was* mine, but it looked like I had to figure in some damage control now.

Ian wasn't chatty on the drive to the Murray house, and I was grateful that he'd given me the time to think. To mentally prepare. To consider what I could say to this spineless little fucker who'd handed over Cara to me last night.

I grunted, shaking my head. "Was it really just the day before yesterday?" I glanced at him driving. "When we came here?"

He rolled his eyes. "Yeah. It really was."

"It had better be the last damn time I have to see his face again."

Like that first "visit" where I demanded the wedding to happen, I pounded on the door.

Ian sighed, lowering his finger from the bell and surrendering to my method of announcing our arrival. "Now it makes sense."

I shot him a side-eye as we waited for that old butler to come to the door. "What do you mean?"

"How nervous they were and what we overheard them say after we left."

I nodded. It did make sense. Shane had seemed willing to cooperate, too scared, but Keira had insisted that *her* daughter wouldn't be my bride. They must have already planned then on forcing Cara to fulfill that role.

And it was that vapid woman who answered, not the butler.

Keira slit her eyes at us, glancing from me to Ian, and back and forth again. "Yes?"

Fuck you and that tone. I pushed past her, inviting myself inside. She bristled, huffing, like that sound would make me change my mind about my attitude.

"Where's Murray?"

She shrugged and sniffed, holding her nose in the air. "Out."

"What do you know about Nora Gallagher?" Ian said, seeming to realize how close I was to strangling this uppity woman.

"Nora?" Keira smirked. "She's nothing but a worthless whore."

"Is she a relative of the Boyles?" I demanded.

She rolled her eyes. "You expect *me* to know about her parentage? It doesn't matter. I heard her mother abandoned her and her father never wanted her. *No one* wanted her for anything good."

"Like your husband?" I goaded.

Her lip curled. "Shane met me well after he'd sent that whore packing. It was never a choice between picking me or her."

"Does Murray know anything about Nora's past?" Ian asked, proving he had patience in droves. I was two seconds from torturing this woman to explain herself.

"No. He never cared to because she was so clearly no one and nothing." She smiled, cruel and slow. "Just like Cara is."

I stepped forward, getting in her face and waiting until fear streaked over her stiffly plastic face. "Cara is now my wife," I reminded her.

I didn't emphasize that as a defense for who Cara was as an individual. I didn't *know* my wife. But she was mine. She was linked to the Sullivan name. To me. And I'd be goddamned she tried to insult anything of my possession.

She nodded, taking a shaky step back.

"Ma'am." The butler rushed into the room, panting and just as out of shape as he was the other day. Alarm showed in every line of his wrinkled face as he looked at his mistress, the lady of the house. "Mr. Murray has been captured. His…" He glanced at me. "His work associates were not pleased with their meeting, and they have decided to keep him hostage until he pays up."

Keira gasped, covering her mouth.

I glanced back at Ian, who wore the same expression that I bet he saw on my face. One that implied, *what a dumb fuck.*

"You must help," Keira pleaded firmly, with authority she was an idiot to think she had here.

I turned, calling out over my shoulder. "No."

"You're family now!"

I stopped, pivoting to face her. "Not with *you*."

With a final huff, amused that she'd try to beg me for help, I left with my brother and truly planned to never have to return.

We didn't get many answers, but I knew we'd get to the bottom of this and handle any problems that might arise.

All I had to do, all I *must*, was knock up my wife and secure an heir.

10

CARA

The two guards, not Declan, saw me to my wing. I wasn't sharing a room with my husband, but that didn't surprise me. If his idea of consummating our marriage meant taking me against the front door, then he clearly wouldn't have any sentimental need to lie with me in a bed for sleeping.

But I was stunned when the guards showed me the entire half of the damn floor. Being in this enormous castle was one thing. Understanding that I had an entire wing—with a bedroom, study, lounge area, and the biggest bathroom I could imagine—took some time.

Mom's house could fit in the "lady's wing", as the taller guard called it. He and another older guy had replaced the two who'd chased me down at the other place, but I was just as wary of them. I'd remain on my guard and cautious here, this new "home" that I was supposed to live in.

"Mr. Sullivan would like your phone."

I whirled around, tearing my gaze from the wide, curtained windows toward the rear of the room. Furrowing my brow, I replayed in my mind what I thought he'd said. "What?" My phone?

He held his hand out, his gaze not as demanding and cruel as his boss, but unwavering all the same. "Your phone."

The other guard stood next to him, waiting expectantly.

"Why?"

The second man huffed a laugh. "So you can't call for help to escape."

I bit my lower lip and lowered my shoulders, defeated by his bluntness. "Oh. So I *am* a prisoner here."

"Your phone." He lifted his outstretched hand further toward me.

"Or else?" I mocked, taking my phone out of my pocket to unlock it and set it to factory reset. I couldn't risk these men or Declan finding out about Mom or the deal I'd made with my father and stepmother, about being paid to marry Declan. The last thing I needed was for the Sullivan Mob to go after my mom as more collateral.

I slapped the device in his hand, and giving it up felt like I was severing a tether I wanted to cling to. This was my only means of contacting Mom. My only method of checking with Oscar that he was seeing to my wishes in my absence. I'd texted him so many times already, and it seemed that he was obedient to my decrees, but I didn't look forward to losing all contact.

"Mr. Sullivan will return it when he sees fit, I'm sure." With that, holding my phone, they turned and left me to… nothing. I had nothing to do. Nowhere to go.

I stood there staring at the tall double doors as they closed them. Stuck in a fugue of cluelessness and simmering anger, I tried to rise above the stress of it all.

Now, I was truly unencumbered. I couldn't focus on following up with the farm or Mom's health. I couldn't browse the weather and see if the animals would be all right for any upcoming summer storms.

I had no way to contact the world, and shut away in this huge but dark wing in an old castle, I was a prisoner.

On the farm, I'd wondered if and when I would ever find an option for an alternative life. Surrounded by the trappings of wealth and a lush private suite all to myself, I sure had stumbled upon one.

But I was just as stuck as I had been before.

That first day turned into another. And another. Another yet.

I saw no one but the pair of guards who'd been assigned to me. Declan never came to me, not to see if I was alive or to fuck me hard for his goal of an heir. Nothing. I was isolated but not forgotten. The guards showed me part of the estate home. Several areas of the castle were locked. The whole upper floor was off limits. Even though they gave me a tour of where I was permitted, like the dining room, parlors, library, and study, they indicated that I was trapped inside.

Through the windows, I saw glimpses of the outdoors. The sprawling green lawn. Ornamental gardens just outside the walls and windows, artfully displayed as the gentlemen and gentlewomen's version of wilderness. Further out, I spotted other buildings, guessing at least one was a stable of some kind.

A pang of homesickness hit me hard as I stared at the hint of such a similar structure. That was where I belonged. Out there, keeping my hands busy, hearing the animals and helping them thrive. It wouldn't be the same as being home, with the herd and horses Oscar and I tended to, but the mere opportunity of being near animals would ease some of the ache in my heart.

I saw no purpose to hiding inside. Wearing jeans and sweaters and lounging around. This idle, delicate lifestyle didn't suit me. This wasn't *me*.

The staff prepared the dusty lady's wing with clothing that didn't necessarily suit me, too stiff and not worn in like my simpler attire back home. I had every personal and private necessity I could ever need, including feminine products. My period had started, as I figured it would, even without the order to track my temperature and use the hormone testing strips that someone had left in my wing. A doctor stopped in, and he explained that Declan expected me to track when I would be most fertile.

I'm not. Ever.

But I didn't say anything. A small part of me worried that the doctor would insist on an exam, but he seemed hurried, like he was there for someone else at the castle. He'd told me to log my menstrual details, and then he was gone.

Who else is here?

I saw only the guards, a couple of cooks and housekeepers here and there, but that whole first week of living here as Mrs. Sullivan, they treated me like I was invisible while they worked and went with ease through the home.

Declan had taken off. His brother, Ian, was gone too.

All alone and wretchedly miserable, I fell deeper into loathing my circumstances. I couldn't leave. I couldn't even go outside, despite the steady gray skies and rain.

I often wound up at the windows, staring out and letting every ounce of helplessness sink into my soul. I yearned for the open, fresh air outdoors. I missed the feeling of drizzle on my face, the thick fur of a sheep under my hand, and the comforting whinnies from my favorite horse as we rode out over the land.

Suck it up. I sighed, pressing my brow to the window. *Remember that this is all for her.*

I swallowed hard, wishing I could see her. To hear her voice. To make her laugh.

Parted from her, I lost sight of the immediate hardships she'd faced for years now. I didn't know why, but being so utterly alone had me thinking more and more about the past, all those easier, carefree times when I was young. Before her body was ravaged by disease and illnesses. How she took me out on the horses, taught me how to fish, and which sheep would be easier to shear wool from. Dinners and picnics. Laughing at silly jokes and picking wildflowers.

Too busy with working and taking care of her, I'd let those sweeter memories fall from my mind, but now, with this idleness, I dwelled on them.

I'm doing this so we can have better times again. Together. Healed and happy. The dream of such a possibility refueled my spirits to tough out this isolation, but it wasn't easy.

After a week, I worried about how dark of a situation I'd found myself in. A prisoner. And a brood mare who wouldn't succeed.

When Declan finally returned, I tensed and wished I could beg for an escape. To run, because the thought of his leaving me but only returning to fuck me filled me with harrowing dread.

At the sound of his voice as he entered, telling Ian he'd speak with him after dinner, I went still.

Hidden in the library, mindlessly zoning out as I peered at a book of photography about Ireland's geography, I waited for him to find me.

"Cara!" he shouted, pairing his summons with heavy footfalls as he searched through the first floor.

I'm not heeling to you, either.

"Cara!" He growled outside the library. "Riley, where is she?"

The young cook I spotted—once when I dared to go into the kitchen for a snack—huffed. "I don't know. I'm not her keeper."

I raised my brows at her tone. He let her talk back?

"Where do you *think* she is?"

"Somewhere around here. For God's sake, Dec. She didn't run away."

"Is she—"

Riley groaned. "No. She's here."

I furrowed my brow, closing the book. *Am I what? What was he going to ask her?* I knew better than to think he cared about my wellbeing.

"Cara!" He tried the library next, shoving the door open so quickly that it hit the wall. His dark glare landed on me, and I tipped my chin up.

"Are you with child?"

I rolled my eyes and stood to put the book back on the shelf.

No hello. No greeting. Nothing. Just a demand whether I'd served my purpose yet.

"No," I deadpanned.

"Are you tracking—"

I crossed my arms. "Yes. My period is just finishing." While it should have felt weird to discuss my body like this with him, I resisted a grimace at what I was telling him.

He'll want to try again. And again. All to be told the same thing. I wouldn't be giving him an heir, but with the deal we'd shook on in the church courtyard, he'd keep trying to impregnate me for the next five and a half months.

I should have said three months.

His face turned stony, rigid with disappointment and annoyance. "Then after dinner, we'll try again."

Fuck. I should've been prepared. He had told me what he needed from me, upfront and honest about making an heir with me.

He must have interpreted my smirk as an argument because he stalked closer, narrowing his eyes. "And we'll keep trying until it works."

11

DECLAN

Not pregnant.

I took my seat and breathed through the annoyance Cara's answer gave me. I was more irritated than I was disappointed. Since I'd only fucked her that one time, I knew better than to get my hopes up too high. I wanted to assume that I could hit a streak of beginner's luck with her. That we'd have a child after the first try, but even I knew how unlikely that would have been.

Now we have to try again.

After the troubling, long days I'd had, I was peeved that I couldn't have a little bit of good news here. I didn't intend to stay in the city like that, but business called. Duty waited. I couldn't spend all my time here with my dick in her pussy. Dad expected me to bring him an heir, but the businesses the Sullivan name stood behind also required my leadership.

I glanced at Cara as she sat across from me. Stiff. Lips pursed. Eyes glittering with green rage. I didn't know everything about my wife, but I was familiar with her sass and stubbornness. She was a fighter—especially against me—and I didn't doubt that she wasn't pleased that

I'd returned. She wanted as little to do with me as possible. That was a given.

Too fucking bad. I'd be slamming into her cunt within the hour, but even that sounded like a chore. I was exhausted mentally and physically from all I had to do in a day and night of work. I wasn't in the mood to deal with her being prickly and defensive with me. I'd told her what I needed. I explained that she was only my wife to be knocked up.

Most times, the fight turned me on. Docile women didn't do anything for me. Nothing at all. I wanted a challenge to overcome, a strong spirit to conquer. But not now. Not today.

The idea of corralling her in the bedroom felt like a chore. Another job to do when I already had so much on my plate. All I wanted after being up for the last day and night straight was to sleep and not be bothered by anyone or anything.

"Hi, Cara," Ian said as he entered the dining room, nodding at her before taking his seat.

She lifted her face, her spoon held midair as she stared at him. "Hello?"

Ian chuckled. Glancing between us. "What? I can't greet my sister-in-law?"

"Oh." Cara took a spoonful. "Sorry. Not sorry."

I glared at her.

"I haven't spoken to anyone in days. I forgot how communication works."

Ian bit his lip, raising his brows as he looked at me. "And is there good news...?"

"She's not pregnant," I bit out.

"*She* is right here." She mocked a sheepish smile. "Oh, sorry. Am I to be a *mute* prisoner and welcome you speaking for me at all times? My bad."

"Enough with the fucking attitude."

She smirked, not making eye contact as she continued to eat.

"Wow. Sorry I was late," Ian said, clearly seeking a way to avoid this terseness between me and my wife. He was born with that innate, so-called charm that I saw as a waste of time. "I just wanted to check on Dad first."

"Your dad?" Cara lifted her gaze to him. "He's here?"

Ian nodded. "Didn't you know?"

"Is that why the upper floor is locked?" she asked.

"What's it to you?" I growled. "He doesn't need to be bothered. The only thing you can do for this family is get pregnant."

"I *am* aware," she snapped.

"You didn't know Dad lived here?" Ian asked, then glanced at me.

I shrugged. I didn't know what Frank and Tom showed her. The guards might not have tried to give her a tour of the whole place. Maybe Dad told them to fuck off and not to have any visitors. It hardly mattered to me.

"It seems meeting my new family isn't necessary," she quipped.

"It's not." I gestured at Ian. "He's my brother. And that's all you need to know. What is necessary is your *making* a family."

"Gosh." She deadpanned at me, tilting her head to the side. "With that sweet charisma and appeal you've got going for you, I'm shocked you haven't knocked up half of the women in all of Ireland yet."

I pressed my lips together. Frustration welled within me, but I couldn't look away. She captivated me. Pushing me—pushing her luck in doing so. And fuck if it didn't emphasize how damn gorgeous she was. Barbed tongue and all. She looked alive and heated, riled up to talk back like this.

Like it gave her a thrill. Her words were intended to irk me, but she had no clue how cutting her comment was. I didn't give a shit about charming a woman, but I *had* tried twice to keep a wife.

"And you're the lucky winner of them all," I snarled.

"Luck." She snorted. "Is that what I'm supposed to thank for this imprisonment?"

Ian cleared his throat. Loudly. "Speaking of families." He shot me a look to shut up. "What do you know about yours?"

Once more, she froze, holding her spoon halfway to her mouth. "What do you mean?"

"What do you know about your family?" Ian asked.

I narrowed my eyes, wondering why she'd be so stiff about his question.

"My father?" She lifted one shoulder and let it fall. "You saw him. You know him."

"You're not close to him," I surmised.

"Never," she agreed. "He sent me and Mom packing when she learned she was pregnant with me. I seldom ever saw him."

"Why?" I asked.

"Because he's a whiny asshole? Selfish and manipulative?"

Interesting. "Is that what your mother told you?"

"She didn't need to tell me. I saw that for myself when I was a child and as an adult."

"Your mom, Nora, just took off with you?" Ian checked.

Cara nodded, and the motion loosened another strand of her auburn hair. As she tucked it back, the simple wedding band glinted from the chandelier's light. "Yes. I think she realized that he was affiliated with the Mob and wanted to run from him. He kicked her out anyway, wanting to date Keira, and they married."

"You were estranged your whole life?" I asked.

She smirked. "Oh, you care?"

I glowered right back. "No."

"We never saw him, other than one time when I was a teen and I was hurt and needed medical care not available in our village. She went to the city to demand that he pay for my medical care. It was the *only* time she ever asked anything of him."

Ian and I shared a look.

So, she was poor. Whatever life she led with Nora was one of poverty.

"And Shane stepped up then?" Ian asked.

Cara nodded. "Mom threatened to tell Keira that he was still talking to her, to make her think he was cheating on her. Keira always seemed so obsessed about fidelity, like she worried that my dad would stray."

"What do you know about your mother, though?" Ian asked.

He hadn't found much in the way of answers about Nora's parents or family history. Until we could prove that rumor about her being related to the Boyles was untrue, it would linger as yet another issue for me to deal with.

Again, she seemed on edge, scowling at him. "Why do you want to know?"

"I mean, did you ever meet your grandparents?" he asked.

She shook her head. "Mom was orphaned. Left on the steps at a church and raised in the system."

Shit. That would make it much harder to find out whether she was related to the Boyles. Leaving the genealogy research to Ian was preferred, but if it came down to meeting someone and beating them into giving answers, that task would fall on me.

"Why do you ask?" Cara replied, tense.

"Because it was a surprise at the last fucking minute that Murray expected me to marry you, not your stepsister."

She laughed once, bitterly. "Yeah. News to me, too."

Why'd you go through with it? After Frank gave me her phone, I scrolled back to see what text she could have received that day, when she tried to climb over the garden wall. Unfortunately, she'd deleted it. She'd wiped the whole damn device, actually, and I wondered what she could be hiding to be that eager to erase her correspondence and message logs.

I sighed, annoyed that she was taxing me with more questions, more headaches.

It didn't matter why she married me. Her motivations wouldn't change anything. All that I cared about was that she was my wife to knock up.

Ian and I spoke further about business, but we were both careful to keep it simple and undetailed. Cara couldn't be a spy for anyone. She was sequestered here and wouldn't be leaving. She had no means to speak with anyone either, but this was the nature of our lives. Never share anything that could be used as a weapon later. We passed the rest of the dinner by conversing about the estate grounds, and I noticed how little Cara seemed to care.

If she was listening, she didn't find anything worthy of a reaction. If she was waiting for a moment to speak up and complain, I wouldn't give her my attention.

Sullen and broody, she sat there and picked at her food.

Ian stood, taking a call and nodding at me as he left the room. I doubted he'd return, and I didn't plan to linger, anyway. Now that I'd stopped to actually sit down for more than a few minutes, on the go and busy all week, I would get sleepier. The drinks I'd had over the meal would make me even more eager to sleep.

But first...

I tossed my napkin to the table and sighed as I dragged my gaze to my wife.

She stiffened, realizing my concentration was on her. Without making eye contact, she tensed and waited for me to speak or move.

I didn't do a damn thing. Looking at her and wishing she could ease up on this independent, recalcitrant bullshit, I sighed again.

Then she tipped her chin up, locking her flinty stare on me.

No. She was *not* going to make this fucking easy. Even though she knew what was expected of her, she had to be stupid and think she had any say in this.

"Let's go."

She curled her lip in disgust and rolled her eyes. "I'm not done eating."

"Tough shit. Maybe you shouldn't be so picky." I pushed my chair back.

"I'm not *picky*. That lady *just* brought this out."

That lady? I almost laughed, amused. She was so uncultured that she didn't know to call Pauline a *maid*? I doubted Cara had been raised with wealth, but I didn't realize she was this out of touch with the lifestyle I was used to.

"Eat after." I stood, glowering down at her.

With a heavy exhale, she shook her head and dropped her napkin to the table.

I admired her tenacity. She wasn't fighting me for the hell of it. Her antagonism wasn't a show for attention or to *look* like she was strong. This woman, this curvy yet slender redhead, was a fighter no matter what.

"The front door again?" she growled, annoyed.

That's enough. I grabbed her wrist, pulling her toward the stairs to my room. "Cut that shit out. I'm sick of your attitude."

"Sick of it?" She scoffed. "How can you be sick of any of me? You're not here to remember I'm alive."

Alive. While my first two wives are dead? She couldn't know what her words could mean to me, but I took offense anyway.

"Shut up. I don't need to hear you say another fucking word."

She didn't stop her attempts to pull of out my grip, and I locked my fingers tighter on her as I directed her up the stairs with me.

"I can *walk*, goddammit."

Reaching the doors to my wing, I slammed my free hand against the wood and opened them. Dragging her in, I relished her helplessness to overpower me. She was mine to fuck and do with as I pleased.

She grunted, scowling as I hauled her inside and released her.

Stumbling back, she glared at me and rubbed her wrist. "I hate you. I *hate* that I ever considered this deal."

"What?" I locked the doors, working on unbuttoning my shirt as I stalked toward her, forcing her closer to my bed.

"I hate what I had to give up for this fucking deal," she muttered, biting out the quiet, heated words as she watched my hands on my shirt.

"What the fuck are you mumbling about?" I shoved her shoulder, pushing her onto the bed.

"Nothing." She crawled back on the bed, and I reached for the waistband of her jeans.

Chasing a woman was half the fun—sometimes. Right now, I wanted her to crawl to me, to bend over for me.

"What *deal?*" I demanded, sliding my fingers under the waistband.

She clamped her lips shut, seething as she stayed still. Quiet and unmoving. I didn't give a fuck whether she wanted to be an active participant in making a baby with me. It would happen one way or another.

But I'd be damned if she talked in riddles and tried to keep me in the dark.

A deal? What, the one she made with me in the courtyard, that if she wasn't pregnant by a half a year, she could leave?

I looked her over, reminded by the sight of her sexy body that I'd never give up this possession.

Or is she talking about something else?

"What deal?"

"Nothing," she snapped.

Liar. I was sick of her sass, tired of fighting her when I had so many things going on.

I didn't react in anger, though.

I grinned.

I'd fuck the answers out of her. She wouldn't keep me in the dark about anything. Not when I was the one in control here. Just like I always would be.

Cara Gallagher—now Sullivan—would *not* beat me in this game.

12

CARA

I lay on the bed, trapped and cornered as I stared up at Declan sulking over me. His hands no longer gripped me with that familiar, brutal strength he exuded. But I was just as much pinned under the intense anger of his glare.

He didn't move, standing and glowering at me until I felt like a trapped animal. A small, hopeless prey. He was the ultimate predator, staring at me with that intention to do me wicked harm. This would be no sweet lovemaking or gentle intimacy. He planned to rape me. And he would probably take me just as hard, if not harder, than he did against the door of his other home.

What is wrong with me? The question blared inside my mind.

Too many things had to be severely broken with me. Perhaps all those days of being isolated and alone here had snapped me, coaxing my brain to misfire.

As I breathed hard and waited in suspense for him to touch me, I felt a sickening sense of awareness. Tension built deep in my stomach. My muscles braced for him to lean into me. And something dark and twisted in my heart relished it all. The danger. The thrill.

I wanted him to fuck me.

After all that time of seeing and speaking to no one, forcing me to be so alone and listless and idle that I fell back to reminiscing on my fondest and sadder memories, I yearned for his commanding touch.

Somehow, I'd come to need him to ground me.

The last time he unleashed his wrath on me, it felt so damn good. It made no sense, but I knew what was coming. Any time he touched me, I came alive. He didn't let me wallow in thoughts and worries. He forced me to just feel.

He didn't move. He stared at me so heavily, like he was trying to see into my miserable soul. And that would mean something else, something worse, was wrong with me.

Because I'd slipped up. I'd mentioned that deal, and I did not need him to know that my father was paying me to be Declan's wife. My husband did not need the ammunition of knowing about my mother's condition. I wouldn't put it past him to use it against me somehow, and there was no way in hell that I would further risk her happiness and health in some twisted game this man wanted to play.

I was already nervous from dinner, when Ian asked me about my family. I tried my best to mask my panic at the mention of my mother, guarded about why they wanted to know anything at all. They were curious about my past, but I didn't know enough to gauge the threat of their interest. Safeguarding my mother was my priority. Keeping Declan ignorant about her mattered a hell of a lot more than having any orgasm he could force out of me.

"What deal?" he demanded.

I almost shivered at his growl. Why did he have to turn me on to the point of dripping cream with that husky rasp of his bossy tone?

I shook my head, fighting the urge to thrust my hips up to his hand. Damning still, his fingers remained unmoving on my skin. The rough touch of the back of his knuckles so low on my stomach reminded me of what it felt like when he'd stroked his digits over my slit, into me, when he gruffly shoved his cum back up into my pussy that night.

I wanted it.

"Tell me what you were talking about?"

Never. I held my breath, wishing I could beg him to fuck me already. Tension simmered between us, and as he looked me over again, I felt so full of pressure to explode, like my skin was too tight and my lungs couldn't hold air fast enough.

"Make up your mind," I retorted. "First, you instruct me to shut up. Now, you want me to talk."

He grinned, shaking his head like he couldn't believe I'd fight him. "Tell me."

His fingers moved, undoing the button and zipper with agonizing slowness.

More. More. Please. I fidgeted. My body took over, and I felt my back arch in preparation to get my jeans off my ass.

"Tell me."

I growled, glaring at him.

"Do you think this silence is going to earn you any favors?" He wrenched my jeans down, yanking my panties with them. The hit of cool air on my pussy stunned me, and I gasped out loudly.

"Do you really think you have any power here?" He pulled the garments all the way off.

I know I have none.

"Do you plan on holding out on me and winning?" He kneeled onto the bed, his huge body blocking out my view of the room as he crawled up over me, between my legs.

"Do you?" He gritted his teeth, his jaw muscles sliding as he reached up to force my shirt and bra off in one rough shove. The fabric didn't cooperate. The stretchy top and sporty lingerie clung to me, trapping me over my head. He didn't bother to remove it, instead leaving it as it was. Bound in my shirt and the even tighter elastic grip of my bra, I lay flat and helpless. My arms shot up, and my face was covered. Turning my head to the side, I avoided being strangled. I could breathe with my mouth and nose to the side, but I was stuck in my own clothes.

Blindfolded and bound.

"Are you feeling so powerful and confident now, *wife?*"

I wasn't. He had all the control here. While I wanted to fight it, while the stubborn need to claim my independence burned within me, I came to understand how freeing it was.

To let go.

Not to think at all.

No plans or strategy.

Just to give in and surrender, knowing that he'd deliver such deep bliss.

He lowered over me, closing his mouth on my breast and sucking my nipple between his lips, hard. At the same time, he thrust his hand down my body and slid his fingers into my wet cunt.

I cried out, wincing at the dual hit of pain. Once I breathed through it, the sweeping wave of pleasure warmed me from the inside out.

"Who's in control now?" he demanded, pumping his callused fingers into my tight entrance. Each push in had me crying for more. Every bite and forceful suck of my beaded nipple forced another gasp.

Writhing and shaking, forced to the buildup of an intense climax, he played me. Bruised me. Violated me. And forced me all the way to the brink of coming.

He stopped, leaning up from my chest with his breath whipping down on my wet flesh. His fingers remained splayed on me, holding my folds open but not driving his thick digits inside.

I cried out, panting and bucking to make him finish me off. I knew he was cruel, but this was agony.

"You still think you have power, Cara?" he taunted as he moved again.

Not seeing him aggravated me, but when I heard the rustle of clothing, my heart raced faster. I swore that I leaked more juices, imagining him staring at my pussy, soaking wet and wide open for his taking.

"You wanna stay quiet and not answer me?"

The bed dipped as he crawled back onto it. The friction of his hairy, hard thighs pushed against my legs, urging me to spread open even wider.

He shoved his big cock into me.

I tensed, curling forward and arching up at the brutal thrust. He hadn't waited. He didn't bother to notch himself and give me a warning. He slammed in, all the way in, and ground his hips against me to add in an extra rub.

Crying out louder, I struggled to breathe and surrender. My body was one step ahead of me. I was slick, soaked with my arousal. He slid in, stretching me quickly, but I wasn't unprepared. He worked me open, and I sucked him in deep.

But my mind...

I fought it. I struggled against this power play, knowing I'd never have any where he was concerned. I resisted the urge to let go and just tell him what he wanted to know.

Battered between the unrelenting and hard, hammering pounds of his body against mine, I tried to think and remain coherent. This would not be an ideal time to blurt something out. I could not risk losing control to the point that I shared the details about the deal that saw me married to him.

And in the end, I lost sight of it all. Thinking. Planning. Worrying. None of it was possible.

Forced under the wave of painful thrusts and merciless grinds against my clit, I could only feel. Drowning under the need to splinter and come apart, I lost track of what I had to keep secret.

He gripped my tits, squeezing so hard that I wondered if I'd ever lose the bruises and marks there, and used the hold as leverage to ram into me faster.

I lost it all. My sanity. This need to stay independent and not give in to him.

He freed me from it all.

As I came, milking his cock with tears streaming down my cheeks, he severed the ties that kept me suffering in my mind.

I gave in and rode the tide of pleasure, so hot and hard-earned after the painful and torturous wait.

I wasn't alone. He followed me, spilling his hot cum into me as his dick twitched and speared up even higher, as if he feared any minuscule gap between our bodies would allow a drop of his semen to escape.

"You're not," he growled, breathing hard as he released my breasts. "You will never have power. Not as my wife."

I sobbed, so overwhelmed with the ecstasy of coming that hard. I didn't care what he said. I wasn't able to *think* yet.

"And you will be wise to forget about keeping a single fucking secret from me."

He pulled out, and again, he thrust the dribbling cum back into my pussy.

A long, low groan left my lips at his fingers sliding in along my sensitive flesh.

"All you're here for is to give me what I want," he reminded me as he stood, his weight off the mattress causing me to shift.

"Nothing more."

13

DECLAN

Cara didn't stay in my room. After she scrambled upright, shoving her shirt and bra down so she could see, she avoided making eye contact with me. Without any energy to push her any further for the moment, I headed to the bathroom to clean up.

She left. I heard the door close while I remained in the shower, and I debated going after her.

My plan was to withhold her orgasms and make her tell me what she was talking about, but we'd both lost there. I got carried away by the lure of making her come with how perfectly she responded to my hard touch. And she had lost all ability to even speak.

Fuck that. Chasing her on the bed was one thing. Letting her think that she had power over me to make me come running after her was something I couldn't abide by.

But she wasn't off the hook. I planned to seek her out once more and demand to know what she was mumbling about.

Deal? What deal?

I had no grounds to trust her. Even if I knew her. Even if we weren't strangers and unaware of all the details that made each other who we were, I had too rugged of a past to be able to give her the benefit of the doubt.

Erin lied to me and cheated on me. Her affair was bad enough. Carrying her lover's baby was worse. All her lies and duplicity got her killed in the end. And that was an obstacle to my giving my father an heir.

Then Caitlin. She wasn't any better. She had been my wife for a total of three months before she killed herself. During that time, she'd lied to my face and pretended that she was a woman capable of having this life with me. In the beginning, she'd shied away from me and my touch, claiming through tears that I was too rough with her. She'd manipulated me and convinced me that she was able to handle my brutality, though. I didn't know how to be soft or delicate. I was a hard man, and I fucked accordingly. My dark soul only operated that way.

Caitlin told me that she was competent to be a Mob wife, but she wasn't. She'd killed herself, too afraid to be honest about her mental health. I inquired about her health. Our private doctor asked about her wellbeing when he checked on her while tracking her fertility. When asked, she flat-out lied and gave no indication of a mental health issue. Had she been honest, I would have paid for the best help to get her the care she needed. But no.

Dishonesty was a similarity in the women I chose to be my bride.

If Cara was trying to be my third strike, if she had any plans to fuck me over, I had to learn about them now, not later.

Asking her about what deal she mentioned would have to wait.

Ian found me just after I'd dressed. The news he had to share wasn't welcome.

At my scowl, he shook his head. "I know, I know. The timing is lousy."

"I *just* got back from the city," I told him.

"And I know you need to be here, near Cara."

Not near her. In her.

"But the men are asking for you."

I shook my head, sighing.

Our enemies always preferred to deal with me directly, and the Sullivan men knew better than to try to stand in my place. On one hand, I preferred this because I never minded being the one to kill our rivals and teach the idiots in the criminal world a lesson.

I thrived on violence. And I was good at delivering it.

But on the other hand, after the long week I'd had, I wanted a break.

So much for getting some fucking sleep.

I didn't bother telling Cara goodbye. Conversations between us didn't seem to go smoothly, and I didn't think she needed to be told where I was. All I needed to know was that she would be waiting here for me while I saw through this newest episode of business in the city.

Over the next few days, I realized my wife was not only a presence at my home that I could return to.

She was also on my mind.

Every day and night that passed and I was kept in the city, my aggravation grew.

I still wanted to know what she was talking about with that deal. She made it sound like she'd only married me because of a deal. *Our deal?* I recalled shaking her hand after the claim that I'd let her go in six months. I wouldn't. I'd never give her up. She *would* live and carry my baby.

Did she mean that she couldn't take that many more months of me?

I imagined she might bore and tire of the isolation at the estate home, but I couldn't trust her to know she wouldn't run.

And at any rate, she showed me how much she wanted my company and my touch. So sexy and open, vulnerable and mine for the taking.

I couldn't stop the memories of how damn good she'd felt. How sweet her tight cunt felt gloving my cock. How beautiful her cries sounded to my ears.

I would never tire of the pleasure of shooting my cum deep inside her, knowing she was mine. That she'd never been anyone else's. Cara belonged to me, and I couldn't get her out of my mind.

Not while I met with the Boyles who were acting like punks at my gym again. Not while I tortured a rat who thought he could help himself to a little more of the money we'd stolen.

And not while I tried to sleep at my place in the city, alone and turned on by her memory. Restless and full of the need to sink into her again and again.

And she thought I'd give that up? To surrender her to some sense of independence away from me?

No fucking way.

She'd come alive under my touch. She shivered and trembled for me as she broke apart with her orgasm. Even though she'd gotten to me, driving me with an urgent rush to come with her, I suspected that she *needed* my heavy hand. That she counted on my dominance to get off.

Like an experienced whore, not the naïve innocent who'd recently lost her virginity, she took everything I gave her. She didn't protest when I doled out the pain. Not once did she cower from my touch.

Instead, she seemed to beg for more.

"I can't fucking wait," I grumbled to myself as I got into my car.

The others could deal with cleaning up the rat I'd gutted. I had other plans on my mind now.

And they included pushing my wife. I'd give her more. I'd fuck her harder and try her limits.

Each time. Every time. I refused to give her little pussy a rest until she was pregnant.

Still, as I drove home, I wondered *why*. Why would she have ever agreed to marry me?

It no longer mattered, but I felt duped not knowing her reasoning. I didn't have the patience or free time to get to know her. I lacked that diplomatic charm that Ian had. My brother was at ease speaking with others, but I preferred to let my fists talk for me.

"She hates me."

I did hear her right when she muttered that bit.

"So, why?"

Shane Murray had to hold something over her to get her to marry me instead of Saoirse. As I wracked my brain on the drive to the estate home, I couldn't figure out what.

The man was broke. He had money, or rather, he lived a lifestyle that suggested he was loaded, but he had no power. He had no chance of ever paying us back, and now that the thought of his debt was on my mind, I decided to alter our agreement.

That fucker should pay. He'd shirked on paying us back for years, and even though I'd taken his daughter in marriage, it felt like he'd changed the agreement too. I told him that his debts would be wiped clean, but that was because I thought I'd be taking Saoirse.

If Nora—and therefore Cara—was related to the Boyles, then Murray had essentially fucked me over.

"Not on my watch," I growled.

Reaching for my phone, I called Ian and let it go on speaker as I drove.

"Put pressure on him."

Ian didn't question me, but he seemed reluctant to just jump and go like he usually did.

"He's lying. Or hiding something. I know it," I told him.

"But what does it matter? You've got Cara."

I shook my head. I did. But at what cost? I couldn't escape the nagging suspicion that there was a lot more at play here, and I might not enjoy the details of who was plotting against me and my family.

"All right." He sighed. "I'll send him the message about the debt still being owed. I mean, maybe offer him a discount or something…"

"Whatever." I didn't care.

"Are you heading home now?" he asked.

"Yes." *Time to make a baby. Once and for all.*

"I was talking with Riley earlier," he said.

"And?"

"She heard Cara asking Frank for her phone back."

I rolled my eyes. "Tough shit."

"I doubt it would do any harm to let her have it," he argued.

"Are you going soft now, Brother?"

He huffed. "Compared to you, I've always been soft."

"What does it matter? If I don't have to worry about her calling someone to come pick her up, that's one thing I won't have on my mind."

He chuckled. "Come on. Call someone to pick her up? Like any unannounced visitor would be permitted to drive close to the castle?"

He had a point, but I wasn't so lax to give in.

Deep down, I suspected she wouldn't run. I wouldn't let her think that I'd changed my mind about her flight risk, but now that I had the impression she'd married me with the intention of sticking around for at least six months, I doubted she'd go back on her word.

She wanted to marry me for some reason. She saw a motivation in something, and whatever it was, I bet it would *keep* her married to me.

Maybe she wasn't eager to run.

It wouldn't kill me to give her that phone back.

But this was how I stayed balanced. In power, knowing she couldn't thwart me.

"I'll consider it. Later."

For now, we had to focus on fucking. And I intended to, nonstop, until her belly would swell with my child. Knowing she could take my darkness and ante up to my need for being rough was just a bonus.

14

CARA

I was alone. Again.

I didn't know if my husband understood that it usually took more than once to get a woman pregnant. A normal one.

I had no chance of conceiving anyway, but still, could a man expect to get an heir when he only tried weekly?

Ever since that one time when my mom demanded that my father pay for more specialized medical care in the city, I knew that my likelihood of ever having a child was slim or next to none.

Knowing that I had no actual odds of fertility shaped my views on my future. I never counted on having children, and once I had that thought in my head—when I was still a young teenager myself—I never really let myself get carried away with fantasies of having a nice, big family.

While I stayed in this huge home, this magnificent castle with no one for company, I wondered what Declan actually imagined it would be like to add a child here. Would he hire a nanny? Would he remain aloof to his own flesh and blood and obtain staff specialized to rear him or her? Because the man was never here. Never. He made no moves to stay for more than a day.

At first, I thought it was because of me and evident with the way he treated me at our wedding. I wondered if he wanted to avoid my presence, as though the reminder that he was connected to me in any way was so awful.

Maybe he was simply that busy. This castle was as old as it was large, and it was stuffed with all kinds of very expensive-looking items. The clocks to the side tables. The chandeliers to the fine forks laid out for meals. More than once, I whiled away hours in the hallways and in the many parlors, lazily looking at the artwork that likely belonged in museums. All of it had to have cost a fortune, and I understood that the Sullivan name represented great wealth. And to achieve that rich status, they had to work, right?

You'd think.

I found it ironic that I worked myself weary at the farm, and we still didn't have much to show for it.

Maybe Declan was that kind of a man. A workaholic, and if he was, it wasn't my business because I was nothing but a brood mare. Or so he thought.

One afternoon, I found the slender brunette in the kitchen. Riley, I heard the cook refer to her as. A junior cook. Maid? I didn't know all the titles. I did know that stout woman and the older, grouchy man were the head cooks. And they did *not* like me in their domain. They were either strictly possessive of their duties and roles as the main preparers of food here or they didn't trust me. Perhaps they had to keep me on the other side of the line in this household. Staff versus family. Or imprisoned guests. There didn't seem to be an in between, but as Riley glanced up at me, I hoped she wouldn't be so uppity as to dismiss me.

For fuck's sake, having one person to speak to would prevent me from going nuts.

"Can I help you?" she asked, setting down a plate she'd just wiped dry.

"I'm just bored." I shrugged, hoping that gesture would make me look more approachable and nonthreatening so she wouldn't shoo me away.

Her brows popped up high. She seemed surprised, like someone being bored in this grand home with all needs met would be ridiculous.

"Yeah." I nodded. "I'm so fucking bored."

The start of a smile showed on her lips.

"I used to be a busy person before I came here." And I didn't know what to do with myself now. Other than miss my mom and the farm. Or wonder about why it felt so good when Declan fucked me raw.

"Busy doing what?" she asked.

I was grateful and glad to see a glimmer of intrigue in her eyes.

When Ian and Declan asked me about my family at dinner that one night, I felt like I was a suspect. Like I was some person to torture for information. Information that they would no doubt try to use against me. Facing this staff member, I got stuck on the assumption that she was simply curious about me.

"I used to work at a farm."

Once more, she seemed surprised, smiling wider. "Really? A farm?"

"A sheep farm."

"Oh…" She grinned, and her whole face lit up. "I can just imagine the little lambs."

Yeah, well, you're looking at one now. I felt like one while Declan was the wolf.

"I'm used to working with my hands and being outside." I didn't waste the effort to smile when I didn't feel happy. I bet it would go a long way to make it seem like I was just talking, not complaining, but it felt too good to just talk to someone. Turning my head, I gazed at the gray skies outside.

She glanced around the kitchen as though she needed to check whether anyone would catch us in here. It reaffirmed my guess that the staff had been instructed to ignore me.

"Then I bet you're going stir-crazy in here, huh?"

I nodded. I didn't know if I was half insane from worrying about my mom and wondering if she was okay or from the loss of having a true purpose, like working at the farm. I didn't belong here. I felt like an outsider. And the next five months and two weeks felt like an eternity to get through.

"I have to say that you're a much easier wife to deal with, though." She gave me a silly smile, as though she was giddy to talk so freely with me.

"I'm an *easy* wife to deal with?" I laughed. I doubted Declan would agree. "I'm not *your* wife."

She giggled, not offended by my sarcasm. "I know. I meant the wife of the house." Then she huffed. "I doubt I'll ever get married myself."

I raised my brows and laughed harder. "Ha! That's what *I* thought."

She sobered up. "Well, that's the nature of the marriages in these Families. Nobody ever thinks they'll get hitched, but then they're arranged to do just that."

"Was Declan married before?"

I hated the thought as soon as it entered my mind. I wasn't jealous. The man was at least fifteen years older than me and clearly experienced compared to the virginal state I was in when I arrived. Of course, he had been with other women. Half the time he was gone, I bet he was fucking around. I tried not to dwell on it. Sometimes, I had to force that anxious assumption from my mind.

She held up two fingers.

Twice?

Learning that Declan had been married twice before unsettled me. Was he trying to compare me to them? Did I measure up to whatever his other wives were like? Why didn't they last?

So many questions pinged in my mind, and I didn't want to overwhelm Riley by asking.

I didn't plan to stick with Declan either. He shook my hand that we only had to be together for six months.

"Twice?" I asked.

She nodded, crossing her arms and resting her hip against the ledge of the counter.

"You've known Declan, or, uh, worked here that long?"

"Yeah. I've worked here since I was a kid. Anyway, first there was Erin. She cheated on him."

Wow. "With a guard?"

She frowned. "No. She got with some Italian guy. I don't remember his name. I get lost with all those Mafia Families over there."

I blinked. "She—Erin was allowed to leave the house? To meet this guy?"

"Yeah."

I let my shoulders slump. "Damn. I wish I could go outside at all."

She laughed. "I don't know why Declan is so nervous about your walking around outside. It's not like the guards aren't always out there, patrolling the whole property."

I wonder what you'd think if I told you he took my phone, too. Riley had her loyalties. She worked here. But I appreciated that she was open-minded to talk with me.

"So, first, Erin cheated on him," I repeated.

"Yeah. She cheated on him, got knocked up by her lover, and then the lover killed her because she wouldn't leave Declan but was carrying his baby." She waved her hand in the air. "It was a big old drama."

"Wow." I wasn't expecting that.

"Yeah, then there was Caitlin. She was terrible. I couldn't stand her." She rolled her eyes. "Don't get me wrong. I don't mind talking with you, but I'm not supposed to mix with you, or with the Family."

"Mix with me?" I laughed once. "Like I'm some royal princess or something special."

"You *are* married to one of the Sullivan brothers. Lots of women would envy the security of the Family."

I sighed, planning to agree to disagree.

"Caitlin was whiny. And needy. And such a liar. She made up stuff to get me to talk to her, then tried to get me in trouble. She was just deceiving, to me, the staff, even the Family, and it irked me. I prefer it blunt."

"Yeah. Honest and upfront."

She nodded. "Yes. Anyway, she's gone too."

"What happened to her?" If she lied to Declan, I could just imagine how badly that ended for her.

"She killed herself."

My jaw dropped. I stared at this assistant cook for a minute, trying to let that sink into my head. I wasn't Declan's first wife, nor his second take. I was the third, and the first two didn't end well.

At this rate, I should be counting on my demise any day now.

Riley wasn't done gossiping. "I think that's why Donal—Dec and Ian's dad—was so afraid Dec wouldn't find a woman to keep around long enough to give him an heir."

I shot her an incredulous look that implied, *you think so?*

"And Dec's not… an easy man to get along with. Lots of women are scared. He's so used to fighting and being gruff and just an asshole." She smirked, at ease to talk crap about him. "So it wasn't like he could walk out there and get a wife easily."

I was well aware. I had to be given an ultimatum to consider it. But that was what he got. Karma and all. Riley was correct in calling him an asshole, and what woman *would* want him?

"And I think that's why Declan is so eager to keep you here."

I raised my brows and stared at her dully. "To the point of making me a prisoner in this castle?"

"I think it's a little extreme. I mean, like you said, if you were to walk around the garden or something, it's not like you could get away. Everything is guarded and watched." She narrowed her eyes and winced. "Have you considered asking him if you can walk on the grounds?"

I barked a laugh. "No. And I don't intend to ask him for anything at all. I don't want him to hold anything over me." I was all too aware of how little power I had, and I didn't plan to give him any more of an excuse to wield more leverage against me in any other way.

"Riley!" The head cook came in and shouted. She slapped her hand together in a viscous clap, like she was calling back a dog from a threat.

Riley rolled her eyes at me. Before she turned, she whispered, "Nice talking. We'll find another time to gossip." She winked, and the silly expression warmed my shrinking heart.

I left the kitchen, not wanting to get the young cook in trouble for speaking with me. Back in my own company, I fell into a pit of anger and frustration.

I saw and felt firsthand how much of a brutish asshole Declan was. And it pissed me off to no end that Keira had wanted me to be a bride to this unwanted monster in place of Saoirse having to deal with him.

I was a goddamn sacrificial lamb.

Standing in my room, staring out the huge windows at the clear but gloomy skies over the vast land, I fumed and let my mood sink further and further.

But it's for a good cause. I fought to remember that. I was doing this for Mom. For a better, more secure future.

When Declan arrived, I didn't bother to turn. He'd returned with no warning.

"Cara."

I narrowed my eyes at the windows, not wanting to face him.

The last time he said my name like that, all deep and full of hunger, I was a fool to think I wanted him. My body desired him, but that was the extent of it.

I refused to let him get to me in any other way. Women, as I now knew from Riley's gossip, were dispensable to him. From the first day, he'd made it clear that he didn't care about me. That I was his wife. I was just a body to fuck, a woman he assumed he could impregnate.

"Cara?"

He walked further into the room. His footsteps sounded ominous on the polished wood, but they stopped when I whirled around to face him.

The sooner I got this over with, another round of sex, the faster I could show him that I wasn't pregnant. And he could leave again.

"Yeah, yeah," I drawled, unbuttoning my shirt.

He frowned, watching me.

I kept my voice dull. Bored. Indifferent, because I had to be. "May as well get it over with," I mused wryly, shoving my shirt open more and unbuttoning my jeans next.

"What?" He stalked closer, regarding me with a skeptical glare.

"What do you mean, *what?*" I snapped.

"What are you doing?"

I rolled my eyes, unzipping. "Getting undressed. Doing my duty."

"*Get it over with?*" he challenged in a growl.

I nodded. "Obviously." Damn, he looked different. Tired, but not worn. That stubble growing in on his jaw made him look more rugged, but the new scrape on his cheekbone threatened to make me feel sympathetic somehow.

"No." He locked his face down, showing me a stoic mask as he gripped my shirt and yanked it back over me.

I opened and closed my mouth. *What?* He didn't want to fuck me now? After all those times he'd reiterated what my purpose was?

I warred between rage that he was rejecting me and disappointment that he wouldn't want me. With his knuckles brushing against my breasts and touching my skin, I felt that now-familiar ache of desire for him.

Ashamed and annoyed that I might lust after his body while he could reject mine, I stared at him and waited to know why he was changing things up now.

"No?" I sassed back.

Finished with buttoning my shirt, still not meeting my gaze and chill as ever, he zipped my jeans and rebuttoned them, too.

"No," he said, finally lifting his dark brown gaze to me.

Then he confused me even more, taking my hand and leading me out of the room.

15

DECLAN

Get it over with? I glanced at her, frowning as we walked down the hallway.

Fuck that. I wasn't going to *get it over with*. Not like a chore. Fucking her wasn't a job anymore. It couldn't be after she showed me last time how much she thrived on my rough ways.

Seeing her offering herself up to me should have excited me. Thrilled me. But unlike the first time when I practically raped her, I wanted more of her slow surrender that she gifted me last time. When she was an unwilling but active participant, when her body betrayed her with desire she couldn't deny.

"Let me get this straight," she bit out before we reached the stairs. "You *don't* want to fuck me?"

"No." I clamped my teeth down on my lower lip to hide my smile. She was humiliated. Stung. I was amused with how bristled she was about my telling her no.

"Not right now," I added.

And not like that. I'd be damned if she tried to suffer through it like a lifeless, emotionless doll, uninterested and unattached. Now that I knew how damn gorgeous and passionate she was when she gave in and showed me the depth of her arousal for me, I wanted it all. I planned to take everything from her, and *getting it over with* would no longer apply.

She'd scream for me again. I'd test her and tease her. I would make her dance along the line bordering between pain and pleasure once more. Many times more.

"I don't want to *get it over with*."

She whipped her head toward me, glaring as we walked down the steps. "That's what I'm here for, isn't it? To be your fuck toy?"

I hauled her into my arms and spun her until her back smacked against the wall on the first floor. "You're here to be my wife." Lowering my head, I wondered what she might do if I kissed her. At our wedding, she was so shy. Now?

Her lids fluttered as I leaned in more. "You said..." She swallowed then licked her lips. "You said you didn't care who your wife was. You don't care about me, so why shouldn't we just get it out of the way? Then you can leave again."

I took in her stubborn expression, not a pout but more like a smirk. I fought the need to kiss it off her face.

"Do you like it when I'm gone?"

"What does it matter?" She fidgeted, trying to dodge me and how I had her caged to the wall. "You'll do with me as you please, no matter what."

"Do you?" I asked, moving my head closer to rub along hers. My lips brushed over her cheek, up toward her ear as I wedged my leg between hers. Pushing my thigh up to her core, grinding lightly, I sucked on her earlobe. "Or do you miss me?"

She grunted a rude laugh. "What's there to miss?"

I pushed my thigh harder between her legs, giving more friction to her clit. "You tell me."

"You want to know what I miss?" she challenged hotly, shoving me back.

I grinned at her breathing hard, already so turned on from just that slight tease.

"Not being a prisoner. Being outside. Staying busy and not idle like this." Her eyes glittered with anger, and I swore she was the sexiest, feistiest woman on earth.

"So when you say you want to get it over with, what are you in a hurry to do instead?" I smirked. "Stare out the windows and be moody?"

"It's better than looking at *you*. Especially when you think it's cute and funny to play games with me and reject me for the one thing you do want from me."

I shook my head. "I'm not rejecting you." I stepped closer, cupping her and pressing my palm to her mound. "I *will* fuck you." I lightly slapped her there before breaking away. "But on my terms, Wife."

She snarled. "Whatever you say, *Husband*."

I chuckled, taking her hand again. "Now you're getting the hang of it."

I wouldn't tell her why I wanted her to want it with me, not act bored. Nor would I tell her that I was struck with this stupid, nagging need to know more about her.

Like what could have happened to harden her into this exquisite and strong woman who'd just take her lot, roll over, and suffer through sex just to get it over with. So boldly, without backing down.

I wanted to admire her strength. I sought more insight for how she could be able to accept her fate, no matter what.

But deep down, seeing that indifference in her eyes and knowing she saw me as nothing but a source of obligation, I was aware of how badly I wanted her to desire me back.

She did. She was capable of getting over herself to want me. Last time, she showed me how, and it was glorious.

She had given me a taste, and I wanted to feast on her submission every single time now.

"Did Frank or Tom show you around?" I asked.

A gruff snort was her reply. "A little late to playact as a host, isn't it?"

"I'm not your host. I'm your husband. And we—you—live here."

"This is living?" Her sass hit a different note now. I heard the pain, the sadness and frustration she was probably trying so hard to hide from me. I had much to learn about her, but I knew she'd hate to seem vulnerable around me.

"I saw you in the dining room and the library." I thought back to when I wondered what she was up to here. Most of my fantasies were of her on a bed or bent over, ready and eager for me to plunge my dick in deep.

"And my 'wing.'"

"You don't like it?" God, spare me another materialistic bitch like Caitlin.

"It's got a bed. I don't care."

I sighed. "What do you care about?"

"How about the chance to feel the sun on my face? A breath of fucking fresh air?"

I stopped her, treating myself to the full effect of her glower. She was radiant when she fought. In a fleeting, barely-there way, she reminded me of my mother. Annie Sullivan. A rare woman and the best mother, gone too soon. She was never a second to my father, but an equal. I recalled her coming to fights, cleaning up cuts and scrapes, hands-on in the kitchen and ruling the household.

Cara didn't want to commit and take ownership here. I didn't encourage her to, but she'd made her wishes clear in trying to strike a deal to get away in six months.

"They gave me a tour. A limited one," she replied with snark. "Why bother with anything else? I'm just a prisoner."

"Shut up." I took her hand and opened the back door.

She inhaled deeply as she walked outside with me. I glanced back, mesmerized by the sight of her. Peaceful. Calm and happy. Contented to feel the weak sunlight streaming down as she closed her eyes without a grimace.

Beautiful. Absolutely fucking beautiful. Her fingers loosened within my hand, but it didn't make me suspicious. She wasn't fighting to break out of my grip as I led her across the patio. Relaxed and caught off guard, she lost that tension that pulled at her muscles. Another deep breath in seemed to charge her, to renew her soul, and I couldn't stop the wide smile that broke across my lips.

Disarmed by her beauty at the mere opportunity to be outside, I realized how I'd erred.

She was used to the outdoors. Fresh air mattered to her. I'd noticed how uncultured she was—mistaking her utensil use, peering around at the décor like it was some foreign experience. It wasn't hard to imagine that Cara and Nora lived a simpler life, without much money, but how simple was it?

Before she could catch me grinning at her and taking advantage of her happy moment, I faced forward.

"Better?" I asked, amused.

"I will be after you show me what's that way." She pointed in the direction of the stables out back.

I bit my lip. She didn't ask me permission to check out the building where the horses were. She didn't demand, either.

It was impossible to miss the excitement in her voice, though. If the idea of seeing the animals out there could infuse that much pep into her, it would be a crime to miss out.

My wife came alive under my touch, and it was interesting to consider how else she could perk up and lose some of her jaded guardedness around me.

16

CARA

The second we stepped outside, my heart lifted. The simple act of letting fresh air touch my cheeks and feeling the warmth of the sun did so much to restore my soul.

It was dreary. Clouds hid the sunshine. Dampness hung in the air, courtesy of the storms and rain. But I was out. He'd let me come explore, and it felt so damn good, I lost sight of my guardedness for a moment.

It felt so invigorating to move and walk over the grass that I let go of my suspicion.

He didn't speak after I told him where I wanted to go. Being out of the castle was an improvement, but I didn't want to be confined to the formal gardens up here.

I missed the smells of hay and fur. Of oats and even manure. My eyes needed to find pitchforks and saddles, stalls and reins. Everything that I used to surround myself with at the farm back home. I doubted Declan and his staff kept sheep up here. The landscape wasn't ideal this far north, but that big building back there had to be a structure intended to store animals. Any form of animal husbandry would do. It was part of who I was, what I did. Out there, I would feel like a semblance of my former self.

My single, unmarried self.

We walked side by side in the open, and I marveled in the vast reach of the Sullivan lands. Our shoes squished in the wet grass, and I wished I could've been wearing sandals instead, to better feel the cool dampness of the rain soaking the lawn.

Over a manicured, trimmed field that extended from the formal gardens that hugged the castle, we took a maintained path leading to the barns. Not one, but a few.

Amazing. An entire outfit waited out here. A full operational business, and I couldn't help but envy it all. No busted walls or chipping paint on the outbuildings. All the windows were intact, the trims matching. Even this lane we walked on, it was smooth and free of mud and ruts.

Declan's family could afford anything, inside the castle and out. I'd never come close to having that sort of financial freedom and success at Mom's sheep farm. Seeing the evidence of the Sullivans' wealth and success burned a fire within me.

I want this. I want this for Mom. One day, I'd make it happen, where Oscar wouldn't harp on me to hire help and afford all the bucket-list items that would make our workdays better and more productive.

Even though this barn and the route to it showed signs of established and older stables and barns than what I'd left at home, it reminded me of it with such a deep, piercing slice of pain that my heart could barely take it.

Over two weeks now, I'd been away. Swept from my life and thrust into a very different existence. Hearing the distant sounds of horses soothed me, serving as a pointed connection between my past and present.

All those long days and nights, I'd suffered alone and without any direction in my life.

And now I was rewarded with this visit to the stables.

I narrowed my eyes. "Why are you pretending to be so nice to me?"

Declan didn't answer, seeming to prefer the quiet of this walk. After a long moment, he shook his head. "I don't pretend."

"But you are. If you're not, then you want something."

Before we could enter the stables, he guided me to the exterior wall and caged me in. One muscled arm lifted as he braced his hand on the surface, and with the other, he gripped my waist and squeezed.

Once again, he trapped me to the wall. I saw now how it was a demonstration of his dominance. He liked making me feel small, like he could position and keep me wherever he wanted.

And, once again, it turned me on so quickly that I fought the urge to cling to him, to pull him closer until his mouth could tease my skin.

"You know what I want," he growled. His sinister, smoldering gaze lowered over me in a slow, lusty drag. "And you *will* give me what I need."

A baby? I licked my lips, uneasy. *Actually... I won't. I can't.*

"You kept me inside like a prisoner all this time. Now you're pulling a one-eighty on me, letting me outside and showing me the stables. Why?"

He narrowed his eyes, staring at my lips. "Are you trying to suggest that you'd rather stay inside?"

"No." I frowned. "You made it clear that what I want doesn't matter."

"Perhaps I'm trying to understand who you are."

I huffed, rolling my eyes and glancing away. "Why bother?"

So you can know how to manipulate me even better?

"Are you always this prickly?" he taunted.

"Only for you," I retorted, lifting my chin. "I don't trust you."

He gripped my face, keeping my chin between his thumb and forefinger. "That's the first smart thing I've heard out of your fucking mouth." He moved his thumb higher, cupping my jaw as he dragged his rough thumbpad over my lower lip, tugging it down slightly in a light massage.

I couldn't look away. He'd snared me again, body and mind. I ached already, my blood rushing through me with a trace of desire infused in it. My thoughts scattered. Lusting for my husband, I tried to refrain from letting him see how badly I wanted him to push me. To claim me.

To kiss me.

"Are you saying I shouldn't trust you?"

He smirked. It was such a devilish almost-grin that made him even sexier, more untouchable somehow. "Not when you look at me like that."

"I'm not looking at you like anything," I argued, hearing how lame and stupid I sounded. It was the weakest lie I'd ever tried to stand behind, and he lost his hold on his lips. Smiling freely, I knew he'd won this round.

"No?" He stepped back, depriving me of the proximity of his body heat. "Then what are we waiting around out here for?" As though he were a gallant gentleman, he gestured for me to come with him into the stables.

He was right, though. I had *no* business even considering trusting him. Not with the rabid desire he caused me to feel. Not when my body could betray me with this urgent lust for him.

Because he's just playing games, you idiot.

It stung when he rejected me. I'd stood there, taking off my damn clothes, and he'd passed on my offer. It wasn't an offer. I was living in that house for him to fuck me, and I'd beaten him to the punch, taking the initiative to remove my clothes. I'd offered, and he didn't want to take me.

As I walked with him through the well-maintained and kept-up stables, I revisited the pang of hurt and bitterness. The moment he told me no, I realized how badly I wanted him to take me and fuck me hard, like he had before. While I was dismayed over my thoughts of desiring him, I faced the reality that something was seriously wrong with me.

To lust for my controlling husband. To ache for the roughest man's touch.

I'd lost my mind, convinced that I wanted this monster I married.

If it wasn't sorcery, it sure as hell felt like stupidity. And if I could remember that, I would do well to forget about this physical need to scratch an itch with him.

"Does your mother have horses at your home?" he asked.

We'd fallen into that strange companionship of walking and not talking. By now, we'd covered every avenue and length of stalls, but I liked it better when he wasn't speaking. Broody, maybe, but it gave me a chance to really look around and let all the details sink in.

"What?" I asked, flinching at the surprise in my tone.

"Does your mother have horses at home?" he repeated.

Why would he ask that? "Yes."

"And she is still single?" he asked.

I furrowed my brow, looking up at him. "Yes. Why? What's with all these twenty questions?"

He and his brother already asked me about my mother and my grandparents. This felt like a second fishing expedition for answers, but I wouldn't provide any. It felt too weird. My guard was up. It seemed like he was trying to figure something out, but I doubted he'd ever come out and ask me directly.

But I didn't offer up anything. I was too scared, too wisely defensive about his interest in my mother. I wanted to shudder at the thought of telling my husband about her illness and her need for that kidney surgery.

He couldn't actually care. Since he'd transported me here, he gave me no signs and he made no moves to make me feel like family mattered. Sure, his brother seemed to always be with him, but I hadn't known another family member lived here until the other day.

Declan didn't value family, not if he didn't want to introduce me to the little family he had. His idea of family values seemed more like addressing obligation and fulfilling duties, like filling me with his cum until I was pregnant.

If Declan actually cared about my mother's situation, should I tell him, and if he had a single iota of decency, he wouldn't keep me locked up in his castle.

"I told you. I want to get to know more about the future mother of my children."

I glanced up at him. "Like you were last week at dinner?"

He sighed, looking serious again. "Partly. But I'd also like to figure *you* out too."

"Yeah, right. Good luck with that."

He hummed. "Because you'll only let me see what you want me to see?"

Maybe.

"My mother never married. She never even dated anyone after I was born."

Nodding, he slowed his walk to match mine as I glanced again at a horse in a stall down this way. It was agitated, and I instantly wondered why.

"What does she do?" he asked.

Lie in bed and rely on medications to make her feel slightly human again.

"She…"

I lost my train of thought, wondering how little I could tell him and not invite any trouble to come back to my vulnerable parent. The less Declan knew, the safer she would be.

Right now, though, all I could focus on was how the burly stable hand whipped the horse in that stall.

I ran. My feet carried me faster without any conscious plan to intervene. It was imminent. If I witnessed animal cruelty, I would react.

"Stop it."

"Ah, fuck you, lassie," the drunk man slurred, sneering at me as he lifted his arm to bring the whip down again.

Without my boots on, I was at risk of being stomped on. Those huge hooves could slam down on my feet. The agitated horse could trample me. Kick me. Any number of injuries, but I didn't consider any of that.

After I threw open the latch to the stall door, I ran inside the space and lifted my arm. Holding it up in a deflecting stance, I put myself between the horse, a mare that likely had just given birth with the size of her teats.

"Stop it!" I ordered, talking back again to the drunk who thought it was acceptable to use a whip to the point of streaking a bloody line on that magnificent equine's back.

"No!" Declan roared it, rushing in after me as the stable hand released the crack of the whip he intended to strike the horse with.

17

DECLAN

"No!" I bellowed it again, tightening my abs as I braced for the hit.

Cara ran into this stall to protect the horse, but the sight of her so near danger threatened to choke me. I held my breath, tense and livid, so furiously enraged.

She didn't protest my rushing up to her, and even though she'd bravely put her arm up to take the whip lashing to spare the horse, I was taller. I raised my arm, not only deflecting any strike but also pushing forward to counter the hit.

I caught the stable hand by surprise. He stumbled in his clumsy step, and the loss of his balance threw off his upraised arm. The whip didn't fly forward. Instead, I was quick enough to push the fool back hard enough that his head smacked on the wood beams of the stall wall.

"Shh. Easy. Easy."

Cara had already pivoted. Giving the horse all her attention, she spoke confidently and calmly, reaching up to smooth her hand over the animal's back as it panicked from the commotion in the tight confines of its stall.

"What the fuck were you doing?" I yelled, unsure who I was asking, this stable hand who reeked of booze or Cara who nudged her foot at me and shot me a stern look.

"Quiet. Stop yelling. You'll scare the horse more," she cautioned, scolding me.

The horse bucked and kicked, frantic and not at ease.

I doubted my yell could be worse than the line of blood from the man's whipping, but now wasn't the time to argue with my wife. Not like this.

Still, I reached out for her to pull her back to safety, but she jammed her arm back at me, warding me off.

"Stop," she said as the stable hand stood again.

"What's… Huh?" he slurred as he tried to remain upright.

"You fucking bastard." I grabbed the front of his shirt and hauled him up clear enough to punch him. And again. And again. Other stable workers ran up to see what was going on, and I practically shoved the man at him.

"He's drunk."

Another worker shook his head. "Using a whip on her?"

They cursed and grumbled, dragging the man out of the stall. I'd let them deal with him. As I turned back ready to remove Cara from the stall, I stopped short.

She'd soothed the horse. No longer kicking and frantic with wide-open eyes of fear, the animal shook her mane lightly and nickered gently.

"Easy," Cara cooed, calming the big horse like she'd done it a hundred times before. Maybe she had. I had no fucking clue. All I could tell was that she wasn't afraid to approach and intervene. More than that, she was skilled and knowledgeable about how to handle a fussy horse. She held a strip of fabric to the worst depth of the whipping gash, rubbing her hand over the horse's side as she compressed the wound.

"What in the fuck is going on here?" I demanded, keeping my tone low and as natural as possible. It felt impossible. I was furious. Livid. So damn mad—that the stable hand had resorted to hurting the horse, that Cara threw herself into danger without a second thought, and that she had the gall to tell me to be quiet.

"Shh."

I narrowed my eyes, daring her to issue that to me, not the horse.

"Cara," I repeated.

"It'll be fine," she said, but I didn't know what she was talking about. Again, I mistook her speaking in a reply to me, but she was addressing the horse, soothing it further with her sweet, firm voice.

I watched her, amazed and confused. I'd never seen a woman in the stables, much less my wife. Erin hated being outside at all. Caitlin was too skittish and nervous to be near any animals.

But Cara?

I marveled in her patience, seeing firsthand that she had a big heart. And she knew her way around animals. Around this horse, like she'd done it many times before.

"Cara." I tugged her back as the stable's main vet on staff entered the stall to take over tending to the wound.

She was reluctant. I could tell she wanted to remain with the horse, but one look at me convinced her to leave the stall.

As we walked away from the area, leaving the building altogether, I looked her over in a new light. I already assumed she wasn't scared to take risks. But running in to save a panicked animal from harm required a *lot* of gumption.

She was selfless, I realized, and I hated that she could be so giving at the cost of her own safety.

"What?" she snapped, proving that she wasn't impervious to my stare on her. "Why are you looking at me like that?" She lifted her hands, checking them. "I don't think there's any blood on me."

"You could've been hurt."

She shrugged, smirking at me as we walked back toward the house. "So? I'm not pregnant right now. What does it matter?"

I gritted my teeth, pissed at her reply. I hated that she'd even think that, much less say it. I couldn't lose the thought that she *did* matter. Maybe as more than just a woman to give me an heir.

"Tell me more about yourself, Cara." It seemed safer and more normal to make a demand of her rather than to open up and confess how quickly she was coming to matter. First, she'd blown me away when I fucked her last week. Then, I fell into the habit of thinking about her and missing her submission, wishing for it again. Now, I had a deeper look into what kind of a generous, compassionate woman she was to protect an animal.

"It doesn't matter. It's not going to make a difference whether you know a million little facts about me or you delegate me to be a figure in your home."

"Don't tell me what matters and what doesn't. I'll decide that."

She shook her head, gracefully walking through the wet grass. "You've made it perfectly clear that I'm nothing more than a brood mare. A vessel. A body to carry your heir."

At the double doors to the house, she pushed inside with pent-up anger. "So, like I said before, you may as well get it over with and then disappear again."

Is that what she thinks? That I want *to leave after fucking her?* I had to work and tend to business. If I had the choice, I'd lie around with her wrapped around my dick all day long.

Annoyed that I *wanted* to fuck her not only for an heir but to sample her submission again, I hurried after her as she rushed up the stairs. She wouldn't have the last word.

"Disappearing?" I snapped.

She shot me a look as she walked up the stairs.

"I disappear to do business."

Her hand shot up. "I don't want to know."

"And my so-called disappearing acts are good for you, too."

We reached the top of the stairs. She'd go to the right to her wing, and I'd go straight to mine. At a stalemate, we faced each other off here.

"What?" She shook her head.

"My wives don't tend to last long," I deadpanned. "Especially when they're in my company."

And it was true. After Caitlin died, I asked Dad if I could just hire a hooker and knock her up for an heir. He said no, that it had to be someone within the Mob world. And that was that. Besides, I doubted even a hooker would agree to it. I wasn't ashamed of being a hard man, a killer, but it warded off my prospects.

I frowned at Cara's reaction. I realized she didn't scare easily, but I didn't expect her to roll her eyes. "I'm not going to kill myself," she drawled.

"You know about Caitlin?"

Crossing her arms, she studied me. "Yeah. Riley got chatty earlier. She told me about Erin too."

I rubbed my jaw, hating that Cara would see how much I needed her to stick now. I didn't want her to ever think she could hold anything against me. Realizing that I was coming to… like her was bad to begin with.

"Caitlin preferred death over being my wife."

She narrowed her eyes. "While I'm inclined to admit you *are* an asshole, I suspect she might have had more reasons than that."

"But I'm not bad enough to scare you off?"

"Like I've had a choice? You only let me outside just now." She pressed her lips together, looking at me seriously. "Besides, I've got too much to worry about to bother with something like taking the easy way of escaping life."

I didn't understand. She had nothing to do here. She didn't have to work. She wasn't forced to do anything except welcome my cock into her pussy and hope my cum stuck enough to make a baby.

Her wording, and the sober tone, made me realize that she'd suffered before. She'd struggled through life to shape that hard, jaded comment. As I let that fact sink in, I wished it weren't so.

Something got to me about this woman, bold and beautiful, and brave too.

What's your real story, Cara?

I wouldn't waste my time asking. Being with her and *not* fucking her was a test to my patience.

The more that she let me unravel layers of who she was, I grew excited about what else she might expose. I wasn't banking on trust. I wouldn't get my hopes up for any real friendship, but something had shifted between us today.

"Cara."

She lifted her chin, sassy and sure. "Hmm?"

"I don't want to *get it over with*."

Her lips parted as she stared at me. Curiosity flared with a hint of desire.

I slid my hand around her slender waist, curvy and substantial. Perfect to hold on to. Her face lowered as she registered how I'd stepped into her space.

With her hooded lids, she gazed up at me, almost shyly.

"Because I intend to enjoy you, too." I licked my lips, and my dick hardened at her troubled gaze locking on that motion.

I walked her back, relishing her awkwardness as she reached out to hold on to my upper arms.

"You're..." She cleared her throat. Fuck, she was gorgeous when she was angry, but nervous and timid, she was just as sexy. "You've said that you're the boss."

I nodded. "Never forget it."

"So, you do whatever you have to do."

I stopped at the door frame to her suite, ramming my body against hers. "No. You'll do whatever I want you to do. For me." Addicted to the allure of owning her body, of being the one in charge of making her submit and surrender, I inhaled a deep breath. Dragging my nose along her jaw, I relished her sweet scent. All her, feminine, light, and sweet. None of that cloying perfume my previous wives had used. Cara was sweet, innocent. With a hint of the outdoors clinging to her, too.

All Cara.

"O-Okay." She swallowed hard, intimidated at last.

"So if I say kiss me…"

She let out a whimper, reaching up to hurry in pressing her lips to mine.

Too light. Too short. But it would do for the start of this game.

"And if I tell you to get your ass in that room and strip for me…"

She breathed faster, her eyes wild with desire. As she turned to go, I hauled her back into my arms, leaning her into the wall.

"You will do so without any plan to *get it over with*."

Shaking her head, she stared at me with such vulnerable need, I wanted to growl and fuck her right here in the hall.

"Now *kiss* me," I ordered. "Like you want to."

She narrowed her eyes, taking insult to how I'd mocked her first attempt.

Threading her fingers through my hair, she gripped the back of my head and pulled me down for another kiss. Her lips remained parted. That sweet tongue of hers slipped out, tasting my mouth as she closed her lips over mine. And with a groan of pure lust, she tangled with my tongue and dueled with the fiery passion I was already coming to associate with her.

Angling her head to the side by moving mine, I sucked on her tongue and battled for dominance in this kiss.

Fuck, yes. Finally.

Keeping my mouth sealed to hers, swallowing her moans and whines for more, I pulled her flush, then lifted her.

I held her juicy ass, each cheek in my hands. She didn't need my order to wrap her legs around my waist. Her long limbs clung to me immediately. Her arms slid over my shoulders, looping tightly around my neck.

Kissing her—making out like air no longer mattered—I carried her into her room and kicked the door shut behind us.

I set her down, rougher than I intended. There was nothing for it. Grace was out the window. I was feral and ravenous for her, and with my dick this hard, I struggled to walk closer before trying to get my erection adjusted under my jeans.

"What did I tell you?" I growled.

She stood there, wide-eyed with need and panting at me.

"Strip."

18

CARA

"**S**trip."

Goosebumps broke out over my skin at his command. The need in his stare taunted me, and I wondered if he was playing with my head.

He wanted to enjoy me. That was what he just told me in the hallway. It sounded like a dare. A challenge. An invitation to *make* him feel good while fucking me.

I knew he enjoyed it. I felt him twitch deep inside me twice now. Both times he'd fucked me hard, he came.

"I thought I already tried that," I argued, too stubborn to just give in no matter how much my body wanted him. My nipples beaded up. So sweet and tense, an ache took form in my stomach. Already, my panties were wet from his looking at me like that. And the kiss. The second one, where he tasted me and finished the lip lock with a nip.

He crossed his arms, narrowing his eyes. Haughty and hot. Fuck, he was sex personified. The devil himself, all wicked and expectant.

Just an hour ago, I had tried to strip. And he'd rejected me. He'd told me no. When he shut down my offer, I felt lost and confused, hurt and disappointed because I'd looked forward to that sweet release of coming for him.

"Strip, Cara."

Was it a matter of control? He wanted to tell me to do it rather than let me have the power to take the initiative?

I lifted my fingers anyway, beholden to please him. If I gave in, if I obeyed him, he'd see to it that I'd come. Hard.

Nothing was sweet about him, but he seemed to get off on making me come apart.

And that would do.

He watched me as I unbuttoned my shirt. His caress felt like a tangible, hot caress as I removed my jeans. After I kicked them aside, thrilled to have his attention on me like this, I felt dizzy under the heady pressure of power. Of mighty strength. *I* was doing this. His stare was locked on *me*. No one else.

I was the one making his dick harden under his pants. It was because of my actions that he growled and stared like he'd erupt before even touching me.

I'd never stripped for him. For anyone. I doubted it was sexy. I didn't have the grace to dance or even pull off a sultry sway of my hips as I removed my damp panties, wet with my cream.

And as I reached back to unclasp my bra, I shivered at the promise in his eyes.

"Now me," he ordered once I was naked.

I walked over to him, feeling confined with his instruction. Unlike all the worries that made up my life, this expectation felt good. Like a reward. Obeying my husband wasn't a job to do but a treasure to explore.

I pulled his shirt off, taunted with the expanse of his taut skin. All his muscles were so hard and tense. His pecs. Those abs. God, his arms were so ripped and solid, he looked like a brutish warrior.

As I lowered my fingers to his pants, I sank to my knees. Trembling with the desire coursing through me, I tugged his pants and boxers down. I'd felt his thickness in my pussy. I recalled the wide stretch of him filling me.

When his penis was revealed, though, springing out hard and stiff, so long and veined, I gasped. I couldn't take my eyes off his cock, tempted to taste the drops of moisture leaking from the tip.

Why not? I acted on impulse, deciding it wouldn't hurt him if I chose to seek my pleasure too. I'd never taken a man's erection into my mouth. I was clueless, ignorant and clumsy, but he didn't protest when I swiped the tip of my tongue over his bulbous head.

A grunt left his lips, and he thrust his hips out more.

Smiling, I kissed his cock, marveling at the soft yet hard texture. The pulse of his desire. All of his—

I reared back, blinking and furrowing my brow.

"What?" he growled.

"Are—" I swallowed. I didn't care if I angered him. I signed up to be married to him for six months, but I would be damned if I got a disease for life. "Are you clean?"

He rolled his eyes, grabbing my head and thrusting his cock into my mouth, silencing me as he fucked me.

"I am clean. I only sleep with you."

I moaned, turned on by his taste, his texture, and the salty tang of his essence.

"I tested before our wedding, and I wouldn't dare waste a drop of my cum. It belongs in you. To make a baby."

He groaned, gritting his teeth as he pulled out of my mouth. I panted, licking my lips and determined to get more of a taste. Knowing I pleased him turned me on more, but he wasn't in the mood.

Picking me up under the arms, he maneuvered me to the bed. "And you're going to take it all."

Before I could react or agree, he turned me around in the bed and smacked my ass hard.

"Aren't you?"

I cried out, dropping to my hands and knees on the bed. I'd lain in here alone all this time, and I realized he wouldn't use this mattress gently. He wouldn't treat me softly, either.

Heat seared over my flesh from his smack, but after I breathed through the sting, I relished the warmth.

"Aren't you?" he demanded as he got off the bed and grabbed something from a bottom drawer of the nightstand I hadn't bothered to investigate.

I nodded, enjoying the sensation of giving in, of surrendering to his plans. My breasts hung heavily, aching at the nipples. My skin felt tight, on fire. And as I rubbed my thighs together, I noticed the slickness of my juices.

He returned, tying my wrists with a long length of fabric. After I was secure, he threaded the strip over a bar in the canopy over the bed. He'd chosen a spot toward the headboard, and with the slack he gave me, I realized I could still lean over.

That was what he demanded, his hands on my shoulders as he pushed me down.

I was tied up, on my knees, my arms held forward and locked to the bed.

He dragged his hands from my shoulders, over my back, and down to my ass, rubbing harder where he'd spanked me.

"Do you think you can handle me?" he taunted. Leaning down to kiss the globes of my ass as he inched toward my pussy, he pushed me to lower my head to the mattress.

My shoulders ached at the position, but the sweet bliss of his touch overcompensated the hint of pain.

"I've handled it so far," I retorted as he lifted up from me, making me miss the sweet heat of his tongue.

"So far," he agreed before spanking my other ass cheek twice, harder.

Before I'd finished crying out, he jammed his fingers into my wet pussy, pushing hard. It wasn't one digit. It felt thick, intrusive and forceful, and it was just what I needed.

Letting the pressure claim me, I lost all threads on my worries. It was freeing, to rely on him and let him dictate what I had to focus on—him. His touch. His demanding instructions to come.

He fingered me and stretched me, working me up to such a frenzy with alternating slaps on my ass. Knowing he was watching it all, every drip he pulled out of me, was half the thrill.

I arched my back, thrusting up to his touch, shoving my ass in the air.

"So far," I taunted back between desperate breaths.

"Think you want more, Wife?" he growled, sliding his fingers out of my cunt. He didn't go far, dragging his slippery fingers up to my other hole.

I tensed at the idea of his taking me there, but he slapped my ass and broke me out of thinking, of worrying and dreading.

His fingers breached me, stretching slowly but firmly as he opened me up.

And it felt... good.

Tight. Taboo. Forbidden, but so fucking good.

I groaned, feeling the slickness from my pussy. "You do," he taunted. "You want more." He slid his arm under me, banding it over my stomach as he pushed his finger up my ass.

Pulled upright, his arm locked over my stomach, his back braced behind me, his digit playing with my hole, he repositioned me until I was on my knees.

My arms stung with the binding. Blood drained down as my hands remained over my head, but I leaned back against him, pushed so close to an orgasm as he shoved his cock into my pussy.

His fat dick slid in. One deep, long, steady thrust into me. It felt tighter, harder, and I knew it was because of his finger still in my ass.

"More?" he growled again, leaning closer to kiss my neck. As soon as he added another finger and pumped into my pussy at the same time, he sucked on my flesh.

I cried out, lost to the overwhelming dual sensations of being so full.

Seesawing his fingers and dick, then pumping into me in sync, he fucked me hard in both holes.

Fast. Gritty, and without mercy.

"Good girl," he praised, breathing hard as he rocked into me. "You're a good girl. Take it all."

I sobbed, so desperate to break apart on him and drown in that release, so close but so far.

"Take my dick," he ordered, thrusting faster and driving me upward.

"Squeeze my fingers." He pushed them in further, holding them in place.

"Fuck." He grunted as my orgasm hit me. "Just like that."

I leaned against him, snapping as my orgasm hurtled through me and tossed me into euphoria. My nerves sang with pleasure. My nipples ached with the pinprick sensation of coming at last. All through my body, I surrendered to the doubly stuffed openings that he'd mastered and played so perfectly to force me to come.

Floating on bliss, trembling as waves of my orgasm swept through me, I felt him pound into me once more and growl deeper. His muscles locked and tensed around and behind me as he held me against him. And like every other time, he shot his cum deep inside me.

For several long moments, he held me, giving us both a chance to come down from the high. I went lax against him, uncaring whether I passed out upright, but he took care of that position. He slipped out of me, and I wasn't disappointed. He used his free hand to shove his cum back up into me before he climbed off the bed. A quick maneuver of his fingers released the binding on my wrists, and I slumped down to the bed.

Spent. Exhausted. And so blissfully free.

By the time he cleaned up and returned to me, I was half asleep. When the bed dipped, I dreamily wondered whether he was collecting his clothes or settling in to stay.

He did. He remained with me, spooning me. Holding me close, he slept in my bed with me all night long.

As I drifted in and out of sleep, I struggled to understand why.

19

DECLAN

I woke up to Cara's warm body pressed flush against mine, every soft and naked inch of her against me under the covers.

In the middle of the night, I woke up and checked my phone, finding messages from Ian and a couple of other men. They suggested that I was needed to deal with business, but I couldn't give a shit. For the first time, I felt like indulging in staying right here and keeping close to my wife.

I couldn't give a damn about going to the city. Now that I was here, I planned to stay for at least a few days.

Even though I took her last night, I was stuck under the need to have her again. And again. That was why I woke up hard and eager for her, sliding into her from behind while she slept in.

The moment she came to and woke fully, she wrapped her arms up around my neck and held on tightly as I thrust into her.

Her familiarity with me shouldn't have mattered. Her lack of protest shouldn't have made me smile.

"What's going on?" she purred, her eyes still closed.

I growled at the needy, mildly curious tone of her sleepy, dreamy voice.

Seeing her smile yesterday, so thrilled to have fresh air and sunshine, would be a memory that would stick in my mind for a long time. Hearing her drowsy and relaxed in bed with me like this was another memory that I would hold on to forever.

"I'm telling you good morning," I replied, grabbing hold of her breast, and she leaned more onto her side and welcomed me in.

She moaned at the deeper angle, arching back to me. Once I found her nipple and pulled it between my finger and thumb, her face broke into a wide smile of pure satisfaction.

This woman. She was a rare gem that I hadn't counted on finding. Not only did she take what I gave her, but she reveled in it.

I didn't want to leave her. How could I when I was becoming this addicted?

We came together moments later, and I figured it wasn't such a hardship to stick around. Other people could handle some of the businesses. I had personally selected and trained the staff at the gym. I had no fights scheduled for myself in the near future. Besides, being near my wife would get me closer to having an heir.

That was the goal, right?

No matter that I was starting to care about her. Regardless of the fact that I wanted her for more than filling her with my cum. Her purpose remained the same. She had to give me a child. And she would. But that didn't preclude me from enjoying myself while I was at it.

I desired my wife. I wouldn't deny it, but it was the first time I could admit that. It was the first time that thought didn't seem ridiculous.

Cara mattered. But I wouldn't be so stupid as to let her realize it.

We showered together, and by the time we went downstairs for a late breakfast, we'd fallen back into our normal state of arguing. While I wanted to take her right back upstairs and fuck her again, I wanted to see that moment of happiness that she'd revealed to me outside.

She'd seemed so alive, more at home outside and near the animals.

I had a hunch that she was happiest out there, and if I could make her happy, then it was all the more power to me. It felt good to provide a source of pleasure—independent and different from what I gave her in bed.

She was a prisoner in my life, but she didn't have to be shackled inside my home. If she was more agreeable with a chance to be content in my absence, I saw nothing wrong with that.

So, once we changed and I led her outside, I watched her guardedness slip away the closer we got to the stables. Then when I told her we were going out for a tour of the property here—horseback—she loosened up even more. I could tell she was too cautious to let me see how excited she was, but I noticed. It was impossible for her to hide her reactions and resist smiling.

"When did you learn to ride?" I asked as the stable hands saddled up a couple of horses for us.

She furrowed her brow, watching the man. "No. Hold on." Stepping forward, she corrected and changed the straps to a more secure knot. "There."

He nodded, sheepish a bit at having to be corrected.

"What'd you say?" she asked, coming back to my side.

I shook my head. "Never mind." It didn't matter. She knew how to handle horses better than my staff did. That told me enough.

"Oh. When I learned to ride," she said, still watching the stable hands. "Um, when I was five? Maybe six?"

"Your mother provided lessons?"

She shook her head. "Well, I guess."

I imagined that wouldn't be an option. She'd given me the impression that she'd lived a hard life, one with poverty and not wealth. How could Nora have afforded horse-riding lessons?

There was still so much that I didn't know about this sensual, defensive woman, and I hoped that this ride would provide a chance for me to rectify that as much as possible.

I hadn't counted on her authority, though. More than once, before we could even mount our horses, she corrected more of my staff. Little things, it seemed. But she knew what she was talking about. No employee of the Sullivan organization could be called an idiot. I expected the best. Ian did too. All of the direct leaders and supervisors beneath us also held up the same standards.

These men in the stables and barn weren't incompetent, so for Cara to be able to offer better advice, it proved that she'd dealt with animals a lot.

We rode out together, and I filled the quiet with an explanation of the land we owned here. It was vast, and I stuck with only a summary of so many details about our property. She seemed interested in the historical aspects of it too, but overall, she listened more than she spoke up and asked in-depth follow-up questions.

Weaving around trees, we stuck to an established path. In the open fields, we let the horses pick up speed and exercise their legs. When I wasn't pointing out landmarks and other features that marked the boundaries of the Sullivan land, she asked about the stables, if we hunted, if we bred racing horses, and if there was any form of a crop nearby.

I didn't know all the details, but I bet a conversation with my father would answer many of her inquiries. I wasn't sure when to let her meet him. He was so fragile and cranky.

Like she wouldn't be able to handle his grumpiness. She tolerated me, and I was worse.

It seemed more appropriate to wait until Ian—or someone in the family—could prove that Cara and Nora weren't descendants of the Boyle family.

Plus, it would please Dad to have him meet Cara when she could attest to carrying the heir he refused to die without.

Soon. I'd arrange for her to meet him soon.

"As long as you are careful," I said once we stopped at a clearing high up on a woodsy hill, "you can ride wherever you want on the property."

"As long as I am careful?" she mocked.

I didn't reply. We both knew she was more of an expert with horses than I was.

"If you want to ride, fine. A guard at the border will know if you're trying to run."

Gazing out at the vast landscape, she sighed and shook her head. "No. I won't run." She faced me, serious and calm. "I told you that I would be your wife for six months. And I will. I always stand by my word."

I don't. I narrowed my eyes, reminded again that she was still only willing to put one foot forward and brace the other one to escape.

"That was our deal," she added. "The one we shook on at the church."

I knew which one. It didn't change the fact that I'd lied.

"Is that what you meant the other day? When you grumbled about sticking to a deal?"

She furrowed her brow and looked out to the distance again, clamming up. Her instant silence unnerved me, making me suspicious.

"Yes. The deal you and I made. That you'd let me go if I'm not pregnant within six months."

Not happening. I walked closer to her, standing behind her as I looked out over the sweeping hills and meadows below. "Where would you go?" I couldn't shake this nagging doubt that she had something else in mind. That she wasn't talking about the supposed deal we had, but something else was motivating her.

I had no intention to ever let her leave. And I hated the idea of her being motivated to leave.

"Where would you go after six months?" I asked again when she didn't reply.

"Back to my mom." She sighed. Her shoulders heaved up and down, and I couldn't hold back from reaching out and massaging her there. Keeping my fingers digging in, I kneaded the tension there, rewarded when she leaned back toward me.

"She's probably missing me badly," she admitted, honest but cautious to open up like that.

"Would it make you happy if I gave you your phone back? To contact her?"

She leaned back, smirking. "Oh, my happiness matters now?"

I tugged her fully into my embrace, kissing her long and hard as I lowered one hand to cup her between her legs. She hissed, jolting a bit at my touch.

"Sore?" I teased.

She rolled her eyes and tried not to smile. "Maybe."

I massaged her there, locking my gaze on hers. "I wondered if being on a saddle would hurt…"

"I'm used to it." She frowned. "Being on a saddle. Not…"

I growled, kissing her again at the reminder that she was mine. I was her first and last. She'd come a virgin, and she would never leave me to be another man's to fuck or pleasure.

All mine.

She wasn't lazy. Eager and determined, she kissed me back as I unzipped her shorts and pushed them down.

"Here I was thinking I'd already proven to you that I *do* want to make you happy," I whispered against her lips as I fingered her.

Breathing quicker and trying to reach up to kiss me at the same time she tried to free my erection from my pants, she whined a sexy mewl.

"Yeah. Like that, you do."

I couldn't picture her away from me, from this place. She belonged here, hungry for my cock, unafraid to go for it and to let me in as hard as I wanted.

I guided her to a tree and turned her around. "Bend over. Show me that ass."

She did, and I slammed into her. Pressed up against the tree, her hands on the wet bark, she braced herself for a quick fuck.

"Harder, Declan. *Harder.*"

Fuck. I gritted my teeth. She'd never said my name like that. Never said it at all, maybe. And it was all I needed to unleash on her. I rammed into her until we were both ragged and worn. If her pussy wasn't sore before, it was now.

Moaning and sated with her orgasm, she went easily into my arms as I pulled her up afterward. Turning her so I could kiss her sassy lips, I kept her close and pushed my fingers into her pussy, shoving my cum back up.

She sighed, kissing me back until I released her.

Then I surprised her, earning a raised-brow expression of shock after we righted our clothes.

Pulling her phone out of my pocket was the last thing she expected.

If having a way to contact her mother would be a compromise that kept her happy, I could make that sacrifice.

"Why?" she asked as she took it.

"I wouldn't want anyone to tell me I couldn't speak with my father." I shrugged, feeling vulnerable to give in to her at all. That I *wanted* to give in. "You can contact your mother. No one else."

She met my gaze and nodded. "Thanks, Declan."

I smiled wickedly and lunged to kiss her hard.

"Say it again."

She whimpered, but acquiesced. "Declan," she whispered with her lips a breath from mine, "I think I need more than a minute to be pounded again."

I took her hand, leading her back to our horses. "Race you home," I teased, holding her to it.

20

CARA

My phone burned in my pocket. I'd glanced at it, noticing it was fully charged before I slipped it away. I felt its presence, and I didn't know how to interpret why Declan gave it back to me.

I was happy. I was glad that he gave it to me and that I could have a chance to contact my mom. His explanation was touching, too, that he could be sympathetic to give it to me in the vein of the golden rule, that he'd want to speak with his parent and could recognize that I wanted to remain in touch with mine.

It also felt so strange to be grateful for his permission and the means to make a simple call or text.

Just a couple of weeks ago, I was an independent woman. I decided what needed to be done and I didn't have to ask anyone for permission or allowance to do anything that I deemed necessary.

So many things had changed since I met Declan, and it was a challenge to keep up with the adjustments.

I learned this week how freeing it was to give up control. When he decided that he wanted to fuck me, I knew that I could rely on him to make it so good for me in his dark, twisted way that drove me wild.

I realized that having all my responsibilities taken from me didn't produce the vacation that I thought it would be. By keeping me in this castle, under his control, Declan had taught me that I was not an idle person. That without a purpose, goal, or something to achieve, my life was nothing.

And that was why, as we returned to the house, I felt stuck in a spell of moody gloom. Of guilt.

He had given me the clear purpose of a lifetime. He wanted me to bear him a child, and that was impossible for me to do. That job would not be completed by me. I was incapable of pulling it off.

I've already failed you.

The more that he made me feel for him proved how much he wasn't just a brutish asshole. And therefore, the worse I felt.

I shouldn't have struck a deal with him to secure my exit in six months' time when I knew I would fail him. He'd entered that deal with me thinking I could bear him a child.

I was nothing but a liar.

At the time, I didn't think it was so bad. He was using me for something, and I was using him just the same. But that wasn't the end of it. I was also using him to secure my father's generosity to pay for my mom's debt.

I was trapped in a layered web of lies, and I wondered how much longer I could take it.

If my husband continued to pleasure me, if he continued to show me how good it felt to be connected with him in the deepest way possible, I wasn't sure I could separate my mind from my heart. My body was useless there. All he had to do was breathe and look at me, and I was aroused. The complication lay between my mind and my heart.

Even though it seemed so impossible, I was developing feelings for him. He was showing me that he cared, and I could be honest with myself and admit that I felt things for him in return.

It felt good to know that I pleased him. I trusted my ability to rock his world and make him come just like he did to me.

"There you are," Ian called out when we walked inside.

"No." Declan sighed. "I'm not going anywhere."

"No, no." Ian chuckled as he waited at the other side of the massive foyer. "I know. I just need to talk to you about a couple of things." He tilted his head toward the study, indicating he wanted only his brother's presence despite Declan grabbing my hand and holding it to show that he and I were together.

I stepped back and held my hands up. "I don't even want to know."

"What?" Declan huffed at me. "Ignorance is bliss?"

"Exactly."

He paused, watching me closely. "By now, if Riley hasn't run her mouth and gossiped, you do know what the Sullivan name represents, right?"

I nodded. I'd figured it out the day of our wedding. "Yeah. You're a Mob man. Enough said there."

He rolled his eyes, and I had a hunch he was trying to hide a smile. "And that doesn't bother you? Being married to a killer?"

I arched a brow. "Should it bother me?"

I wasn't heartless, but I had a jaded and scrappy moral compass. I wasn't stupid either. I, like everyone else in the world, knew that organized crime Families existed. I never thought I would be married into such a powerful one, but what could I do about it now? Declan didn't seem eager to kill me or my mother, so that was enough.

"I grew up knowing my father was affiliated with a crime Family." I shrugged. "I knew that my father, half of me, came from a crime Family, and it never made me cry myself to sleep."

Ignoring his brother as he cleared his throat, impatient to speak in the other room, Declan stepped closer to me and kissed me hard. "You don't back down from anything life throws you, do you?"

"Only you." I smiled. *In a good way.*

I wasn't sure what he was looking for as he peered at me. Was he waiting for me to say that I felt uncomfortable to be married to a rough man? I doubted I could ever admit that. I now knew how good it felt to welcome a little pain and hardness, a little violence in my life, and I couldn't imagine going back to what I lived like before.

I enjoyed being with him.

As I was struck with the realization that I treasured being his wife, his woman, that guilt returned.

If I told him that I couldn't carry a child for him, he would dismiss me. He would cast me out of his bed, out of his life.

I didn't need him anymore. I married him, and that action was the stipulation that my father gave me in order to pay off my mom's medical debts. Now that I had my phone back, I was eager to check and confirm that he'd seen to his side of this deal.

Faced with the thought that I wouldn't be here in this castle to see this man ever again, I struggled with a deep sense of loss I never expected to feel. After connecting with him like we had over the last couple of days, I had to remind myself that it wouldn't last.

Uncomfortable with these thoughts of guilt, I shooed him back. "Go on. Do your business."

He couldn't resist pressing his lips to mine once more. Every time that he kissed me, my resolve weakened that much further.

"Don't go far," he teased. "I will see you soon." After a playful slap on my ass, he turned and strode toward his brother.

As soon as he was gone, I went up to my room and pulled my phone out of my pocket. Staring at it, I tried to tamp down the suspicions that arose.

He had to have looked through it. I was so glad I'd reset it to factory settings when Frank asked me for it.

But now... I grimaced, wondering if he was tracking me with the device. Could he know what I did with it?

He'd given me the limitation of only calling my mother, but if I had to contact Oscar, was that so wrong?

I shook my head, calling his cell phone. Calling my one stable hand was like calling my mother. Besides, if she was sleeping, I didn't want to wake her.

And if Declan asks, I'll explain why I decided that.

I waited for the call to connect, and when Oscar answered, I smiled.

"Cara!" He whooped. "I've been wondering when you'd call. My gosh!"

"Sorry, I've been busy."

Not. Other than taking Declan's dick, I'd been bored and depressed. Restless.

"How is Mom doing? The farm, everything. Fill me in."

He chuckled. "How come it took you so long to call?"

"Uh, the reception is *really* spotty here."

He accepted that as an answer. Oscar was always an easygoing guy.

"Good. Good. The herd's doing well. I haven't had much luck finding another helper, but now and then, Thomas pitches in when he can."

I nodded. That was good. Thomas was maybe a year or two younger than me, busy with college, but he probably wanted the flexible means of making extra money.

"How's Mom?"

"Oh," he said, chuckling, "she's the same old. You know. But it was a genius move asking Patti Gehring to sit with her and whatnot. Her husband just got that trucking job, and it seemed like she was lonely across the street. I hear them giggling and chatting all the time from the window up there."

I smiled, breathing easier.

"She's feeling okay?" I checked. As soon as I was finished getting this report from him, I'd call her cell phone.

"Eh. She's got her good days and bad days. That new painkiller seems to help a lot, but Patti said something about the pharmacy claiming it wasn't covered or somethin'. She's harping on them to explain when it would be available."

Furrowing my brow, I walked back and forth through my suite. "Hmm."

That's weird. Lots of medications required a private, out-of-pocket coverage, but Mom didn't have to worry about that anymore.

I stopped, mid-step and tense with instant dread.

Right?

That was the deal. I marry Declan so Saoirse wouldn't have to, and my father would pay for Nora's health.

"Is she home now?" I asked him.

"No, no. Patti just took her to an appointment, and I see she's left her dang cell phone on the table in the kitchen again." He sighed. "But I'll tell her you called. She sure does miss you. I do, too, Boss. And so do all the sheep and horses here."

I nodded, in a rush to end the call now.

As soon as we disconnected, I broke my agreement with Declan. I used my phone for something else, opening the browser and logging into the main debt collection site.

Blinking didn't change what the screen had for me to read.

Refreshing the page kept it the same too.

All I saw were *more* past-due reminders.

Not a single fucking thing had been paid!

Fury escalated within me like a hot, molten wave. I tensed, breathing fast as my heart hammered harder.

"That asshole."

I gritted my teeth, logging out and swiping out of the page to erase that I'd gone to it at all. Then I went back to the call pad and tapped in my father's number. There had to be an answer for this. There had to be a damned good reason he hadn't seen to his end of the deal.

He'd agreed that by sparing Saoirse, I'd secured Mom's debts to be paid. That she'd remain on the kidney transplant list and also be pushed up to be chosen sooner once a match was found.

Damn you. No, fuck *you.*

I turned, ready to press the *call* button. Facing the door, I paused and watched as Declan entered the room.

"Cara." He smiled, lifting his chin as he looked me over.

I swallowed, caught in the act of attempting to break his rule again.

Calling my father wasn't what he'd given me permission for, but I had to know if he'd reneged.

"Yes?" I lowered the phone, tapping it against my thigh.

"You need to get ready."

I laughed once. "You *do* want to keep me sore."

He stalked closer, taking my phone and tossing it to the bed. As he wrapped his arms around me, I gave in to the demand of his lips hot and wet on mine.

Just like that, he pushed me to lose my grip on reality. To forfeit control. To stop thinking about my worries. All I could do was feel him and never want this pleasure, this deep intimacy and desire, to ever stop.

"But you like it," he taunted.

I nodded. "I won't lie. I do."

"Get ready to leave," he said instead as he released me.

"For what? Another ride?" I smirked. "Don't spoil me rotten now."

"Funny." He shoved his hands into his pockets and smirked. Knowing I could amuse him with my wry humor felt good.

"We're leaving for a gala in the city," he announced. "Ian was talking with me about it."

I blinked wide. "A gala? *I* have to go?"

"Yes. I'm expected to show up, and as such, you need to show up with me and show everyone that you're my wife. That we are not going to let the Sullivan name die off anytime soon."

But it will if I'm your wife. I swallowed and nodded. He had me flustered, but I refused to show it.

"Sure. Yeah."

"I'm sure we can find a dress on the way to the city." He glanced at his watch, rotating his wrist and showing me how his muscled arm flexed in the process. "We'll leave within the hour."

"Okay."

It wasn't okay. I needed time to call my dad and demand an explanation for why he hadn't paid for Mom's bills.

But then again...

"Declan?"

He turned back into the room, brows raised.

"What kind of a gala is this?"

"Are you asking who'd be there? Or what bullshit charity it supposedly fundraises for? Because I have no clue."

"Uh..." I tucked my hair behind my ear. "Who'd be there?"

He shrugged. "Other crime Families, mostly. Some government officials. Politicians."

I nodded and turned to find a bag and pack. All the while, I planned to discuss this issue about the debts with my father.

He'd be there. My stepsister wouldn't let anyone fail to invite her to a social thing like this. Keira no doubt wanted to be seen, and my father *was* connected to the smaller crime Family of the Murray name.

It'd be the first time I'd see him since my wedding.

And I bet he wouldn't be prepared for how much I've already changed and grown into an even stronger woman than before.

21

DECLAN

As soon as I exited Cara's room, I saw Ian rushing up to me in the hallway.

I groaned. I loved my brother. I really did. And I appreciated everything he did. Without him, I'd be even more stressed out and overworked.

"We *just* talked."

He nodded, meeting me as I strode toward my wing. After one glance over his shoulder, perhaps to check that Cara's doors were closed, he sighed and pulled his phone out. "Yeah, and a lot can happen in a few minutes."

"Now what?" I asked, letting him follow me into my wing as I planned to pack for the night away.

"I'm tracking Cara's calls," he said, "just like you asked."

I nodded, furrowing my brow as I stood in my closet, considering all my suits and tuxedos. I hated dressing up. Black-tie events were a drag, but I'd be damned if I didn't look the part.

"I gave it back to her earlier today."

"Yeah. The first number went to a man named Oscar."

I stiffened, and he held up his hand to stop me from speaking.

"Who is an employee at the address for Nora Gallagher."

I exhaled long and hard. "So she did call her mother." *Maybe he's hired help and gave the phone to Nora.*

"For five minutes, she spoke with that line. But then, she also called another number. I think she hung up too soon. The call only lasted for two seconds."

I narrowed my eyes. "Who was that call to?"

"Shane Murry." Ian stuck his phone back in his pocket.

"Her father?"

He shrugged. "I got the impression that she wasn't close with him."

"That's my impression too." I had no clue why she'd call him. I hadn't heard from the Murrays since I changed the details of the deal with him, that he'd still need to pay up his debts owed to the Sullivans. Maybe I could press him on that detail at this gala. He'd suffer under the pressure.

"Well, Murray will be at this gala. If she wants to speak with him, she can when we're there." *While I stand right next to her.*

"That's not all." He stuck his other hand in his pocket. "I got an email about Nora."

"What about her?" I rifled through my options, choosing a tuxedo to pack for tomorrow night.

"Whether she's at all related to anyone in the Boyle family." Ian smiled. "She's not. Not at all. Her father was a clergyman from France, and her mother was some secretary on vacation from Australia."

I exhaled a long breath of relief again. "Good. Thank you for uncovering that information." I frowned. "But why did Dad even think that Nora Gallagher could've been a Boyle relation to begin with?"

Ian shook his head. "I don't know, but I was going to check in with him before we leave for the gala."

"I'll join you."

Together, we headed upstairs to the private wing that Dad resided in and never left. The guard nodded at us and let us enter.

Before we even reached his actual bedroom, I heard the coughing. Ian grimaced. "It sounds like he's getting worse."

Which we should expect. "And he'll get worse yet," I agreed sadly.

It put more pressure on me to impregnate Cara. She had to give me a child. It was imperative. It was impossible to try to make it happen before he died. I knew that. But even if he didn't live long enough to know the name would carry on, I would never stop trying.

"I thought—" Dad broke into more coughs as he saw us. "I thought you both would represent me at the gala."

I smirked, amused that even though he was weak and dying, he never had his finger off the pulse of the crime world. With a tablet and his phone, and a lot of communication with Ian, he seemed to always know what was going on.

"We are," I said.

"Your wife, too?" he asked.

I nodded. "Cara too."

"Good. Show those fuckers that we're not letting our line die out."

"Dad," Ian said, taking his usual seat by the bed. "I finally got the answers about Nora Gallagher's parentage."

He raised his bushy brows. "Is she a Boyle?"

Ian shook his head. "Not at all. I traced back her parents, grandparents, and great-grandparents. None of them are related to any Boyle."

His smile was soft and easy. "Good."

"But why'd you think that she was?" I asked.

"Rumors." He smirked and shrugged.

"Who'd you hear it from, though?" Ian asked. "If it's someone at the gala, we could ask why they started the rumor."

Dad focused on me, his rheumy eyes stern. "Keira Murray. That's where my associates said the rumor originated."

Ian and I shared a quick look.

What the hell?

"Cara's stepmother?" Ian checked.

Dad nodded.

I knew Keira disliked Cara. That was evident in how adamantly she foisted Cara onto me in marriage to spare Saoirse having to get hitched with me.

What is her fucking deal? Keira was bitter and whiny, but to start a rumor like that? For what?

I'll find out soon enough. I wasn't above putting pressure on Shane for paying back his debt or on Keira to explain herself and understand why she'd tried to stir up shit.

I left Dad, promising him that I was working on getting an heir. Back in my wing, I packed and prepared for the night away. We would leave tonight, but that was no simple drive.

I planned the security detail, thinking ahead to how many men I'd want at the gala venue itself, too. My men would be with her and nearby at all times. So would I. I didn't intend to let my wife stray from me for more than a single moment, and I didn't care if I was over-the-top with my security.

I wouldn't let anything happen to her.

Not just because she would be the mother of my child but also because I cared for her. She'd snuck under my skin, and if I wasn't careful, I'd be tempted to admit I love—

"What the hell?"

I looked at my phone.

The number was unidentified, but the text sent my heart racing.

I asked Riley for your number.

Is my husband too busy to help me decide on a dress?

I grinned, walking toward her wing. This was bullshit. It was time for her to just stay in my room, in my bed.

Never, Wife.

I pushed open her doors, finding her standing in lacy black lingerie as she held up a black gown from a hanger in her left hand and a green one from her right.

"Cara..." I growled her name, stalking straight to her.

She gasped, running back. "No. No. Come on. Riley found these in storage, said they were shipped here as wedding gifts last week."

I snagged her, kissing up her neck as I tugged at the cups of her bra.

"You said we had an hour to leave and—" She shut up, holding her breath as I bit at her breast then dragged my tongue over the bite to soothe the sting.

"An hour," I agreed.

I took both dresses and flung them to the bed. Then, holding her by the waist, I walked her toward the chair.

I sat, pulling her panties down as I leaned forward to mash my mouth to her pussy.

"Oh…" She threaded her fingers through my hair, rocking into my face.

"An hour is more than enough time," I promised as I stared up at her and fingered her cunt. Creaming up my digit, I then pushed it into her ass and used that leverage to tip her closer to me so I could feast on her.

Enough time for now.

I wasn't sure anymore if one lifetime would be enough for how much I wanted her.

22

CARA

While choosing a dress with Declan's help was… fun, wearing it to this gala was not.

It wouldn't have mattered what I wore. The discomfort that claimed me once I set foot in this posh, humongous ballroom would follow me regardless of any wardrobe change I could have attempted.

I don't belong here.

Among the rich and famous. Next to the influential, pompous people gathered here like stars and leaders.

Or thugs. Now that I'd married a Mob man, I felt confident that I knew the type. It was all in the eyes, that brooding, dark stare that promised pain and death.

Women cast me glances, their disgust evident in their amused smirks. Hair done up, dresses hugging their slender bodies, and so much makeup that I felt too plain. These women were not like me. I would never have the willpower or energy to doll myself up and inject chemicals under my skin to look that fake, that plastic—and I swore for some of them, drugged up and too high, unable to socialize without help.

Tuxedoed men milled around the lavish space. Their bling glittered under so many chandeliers. All their hands bore gems and jewels, expensive watches and hard-earned scars.

These people were strangers, set aside by wealth and purpose as the denizens of the criminal world.

And next to Declan, I wished I could hide further.

He kept me next to him. His hand had yet to leave me. If he wasn't holding my hand, he was touching the small of my back. Then when he wasn't hugging me, commanding my attention on him as he stole a kiss, he was standing behind me with his arm possessively over my stomach as he pulled me back to him.

I wouldn't complain.

His hard, hot body was familiar. It reminded me of the security he gave me when he took control. In and out of the bed. With him glued to my side, I relied on his comfort and ease of mingling in this crowd that I was certain I'd never feel a part of.

Down to my bones, I was nothing but a farm girl. A hardworking, middle-class plebeian. Expected to show up here, I was cast so far out of my element that I wished I could try my hand at seducing my husband to lure him out of here.

"You rub that ass against me one more time…" he growled into my ear, leaning over me as he stood braced behind me.

I couldn't help the shiver his threatening, husky tone incited.

He groaned, kissing along my jawline as he inched his hand over my dress.

Goddamn, was he handsy. And possessive. I wouldn't have been shocked if he was acting like this, doting and attentive, because he saw how uncomfortable and out of my element I was.

Or maybe he was marking his territory, letting everyone see that he'd truly married me and had taken me as his.

No one had come to our wedding. An average-sized crowd had attended the reception. Here, we seemed to be broadcasting our married status to the whole world.

And among the many fancy, cold people drinking and dancing in the ballroom, I spotted *them*. My so-called family who'd wanted me so little that they conspired to force me to marry Declan.

Shane and Keira stood together, seeming to be a couple in love. From a distance, I could tell that they were faking it, acting at ease while their smiles didn't meet their eyes. While their gazes wandered.

"I should just fuck you right now," Declan rasped in my ear.

Are you faking it too? I'd never been in public like this to know if this was how he always acted with a woman. I enjoyed his gruff possession, but he seemed to be laying it on thickly.

Is it an act for you?

I sighed, hating that I could still be so jaded, so quick to assume that he could mean it that he wanted me to feel secure and desired, even in public. The only time I'd had to get to know him were in private moments, so far, usually as we fucked.

This felt like a trial.

A test.

And I wasn't sure I would know if I passed, this first time in public with him.

"You'd fuck me in front of all these people?" I challenged.

"No." He sighed, standing straighter. "No man will ever see your body. No one but me."

I bit my lip. Damn, he was protective tonight.

"Dec." Ian nodded at me, his usual greeting, short and curt. "Smith wants a word."

He shook his head, taking my hand as he stepped beside me. "No. Not tonight."

Ian shrugged.

I didn't know who Smith was, but I was hoping Ian could drag his brother off to speak to someone. I had yet to find an opportunity to slip away. All I needed to do was confront my father and ask why nothing had been paid toward my mother's bills. Just a minute. One quick chat. But Declan seemed unable to let me out of his sight.

Finally, I found a chance to step aside.

"Stay with her," Declan told Ian when he was summoned to speak with a few older men.

Ian nodded, stepping back toward me, but since I saw a man calling out *his* name, I snuck away from my brother-in-law too.

I'd last seen my father near the drinks. Picking up my gown to hurry toward that area, I roved my head side to side, seeking him out.

Dammit. I couldn't spot him. I searched, craning my neck to see past all these people who needed a refresher from the bounty of alcohol here.

Where is he?

I felt so obvious, frantic to find both my father and my husband. I had to speak with my father and get answers. But I also had to keep an eye on where Declan was so he wouldn't come and hover, all overprotective again.

Should I come clean? I'd warred with the option of just telling him all. To this moment, I still couldn't tell whether I was making a mistake in keeping this a secret from him.

What would happen? If I broke down and told Declan that I'd only married him because my father agreed to pay off my mother's debts, what would happen?

I feared his anger.

I worried that it would wound him. Because even though we'd been forced to marry and had done so without love, I hated the idea of ruining this slow buildup of reluctant affection we seemed to have now.

But what if I tell him, and once he knows that my mother is my weakness, he tries to use that against me too?

"Cara?"

Keira's haughty voice stopped me in my tracks. I spun toward her, finding her in a burgundy dress that made her face look even redder. And blotchy. Or maybe that was the lighting. I approached her cautiously.

This woman never had any nice words to say to me, and I had no reason to lower my guard now. "Where's my father?"

She snorted. "Your *father*? My husband has never been *your* father. He's just a sperm donor. Shane is *Saoirse's* father."

I rolled my eyes, shaking my head. She'd always been so spiteful, so determined to wash away the fact that my father ever dated my mother and had me. Like we were a stain on her clutch on him.

"Where is he?" I demanded. I had to be running out of time. Declan would be seeking me out.

"Nowhere you need to know." She looked me up and down, disdain clear in her unimpressed stare as my stepsister joined us.

"I *do* need to know." I stepped up closer, unafraid. "I need to know why my mother's medical debts haven't been paid. Why he hasn't held up his end of our deal."

She smiled prissily, glancing at Saoirse as she laughed.

"Answer me," I said.

Keira only giggled, a high-pitched sound that grated on my nerves and made me even madder.

"We never said *when* we'd pay anything for Nora." She tilted her head to the side, smiling wide, like she'd been waiting for this moment. "It could be... years."

I gritted my teeth, stepping forward with the urge to strangle her. "You liars."

"What, you need money?" Keira taunted. "Ask your 'husband'."

Saoirse snickered. "How's it going, a stupid, ugly idiot married to a rough brute like him?"

"You have no room to talk about me," I warned her. "Or him, you bitch."

Keira gasped. Her hand flew up, and she slapped me—hard. Stinging needles of pain lanced over my cheek, and as my head flung back, my hair whipped to the side.

"Don't you..." She growled. "How *dare* you be so disrespectful to your sister!"

"You—" I lunged after her as she turned and slipped away. Saoirse's lingering laughter floated with them, and before I could weave through the crowd and chase them down, I lost my way.

Further from the drinks area, almost to the middle of the ballroom's center, the dance floor, I stood still and let my arms sag.

"Fuck!" I whispered to myself, scanning the crowd.

I wanted to speak to my father, to demand that he own up to his end of the deal. I couldn't have gone through all of this for nothing. I refused to consider the chance that I'd married a stranger to abandon my mother and not secure her future for her.

As I spun, impatient to find my father, my gaze landed on Declan instead.

With a furrowed brow, he hurried up to me. He cut through the crowd, his eyes so stern with worry and anger.

"Where did you go?" he asked.

I turned to the side, giving him more of my profile. My cheek stung, and I was so nervous that he'd see the evidence of Keira's slap.

"I just wanted to walk around," I replied, defeated to miss out on speaking with my father.

"Don't tell me you need another breath of fresh air already," he mocked. "We just did that fifteen minutes ago."

I smiled, wishing I felt the full effect of his gentle teasing.

"Hey." He frowned again as he reached for me. "What's wrong?"

I tried to keep him toward my side, hiding the full view of my other cheek. "I just want to go." That wasn't a lie, but it was far from the whole truth.

He sighed, still studying me closely. "We will."

"I just don't fit in here. I don't belong."

"You do. With me."

"That's the only place I want to fit." And I meant that sincerely, too. Now that I was back with him, near his powerful body and take-no-shit attitude, I felt stronger. Calmer.

"What the fuck is this?"

He scowled, reaching up to cup my jaw and turn my face toward him.

Oh, shit.

"Are you wounded?"

"I…" I clamped my lips shut as he brushed his thumb over the redness on my cheek.

Gentle. Worried. Soothing.

It was always so remarkable to witness this other side of him that he showed me.

"Tell me, Cara." His jaw tensed as he glared down at me. "Tell me who the fuck dared to touch you."

Furious, too. Can't forget about his default mode.

"Who the fuck hurt you?" he demanded.

23

DECLAN

I saw red. My entire body tensed with the need to kill someone. Not just anyone. The person who'd dared to strike my wife.

"Cara." I tried to rein in my anger. It burned, bottled within me as I fought to speak as calmly as possible. Peace no longer existed. Only rage.

"Who hurt you?"

She shook her head, casting her gaze down as she sighed. "No one."

"*No one.*" I gripped her upper arms harder. "Don't lie. Don't try to tell me that you walked into a fucking wall."

The second I left her, she was hurt. It was one of my biggest fears, that I'd lose her. Now that I'd found her, I refused to consider her being gone. Life was always dangerous. People were hurt and killed on a daily basis, more so in our lives as we dealt in criminal ways of business and control.

Cara was supposed to rise above that. She was supposed to be untouched by any other man, any possible threat.

And I'd failed.

"I did bump into something." She cleared her throat, frowning. "Someone."

"Who?" I demanded in a low growl.

She shrugged, loosening my grip on her. "A waiter. A server? I don't know what you rich people call them. One of those guys in the tuxedos holding up trays of drinks."

I gnashed my teeth together, madder yet.

She was lying. It was so obviously a lie. I wasn't familiar with all her tells, but I felt the deception between us.

Don't fucking lie to me. Don't.

I wanted to believe her, but I couldn't. I longed for a reason to know why she'd try to lie, but this wasn't the time for this bullshit.

This wasn't the place for it, either. I'd be teaching her a lesson about lying to me. That shit wouldn't stand. But I was sick of this stupid party. We'd shown up. People saw us. All that bull crap was over with, and I no longer wanted to stick around here.

I had to see to her cheek. I wanted to make her feel safe again. And more than anything, I had to get to the bottom of this and know who'd dared to touch her, let alone wound her.

"Ian."

He was there, worried and attentive like always.

"Ask the men. Find out who she was talking to last."

Cara flinched but still kept her face lowered. She had to know I had eyes and ears everywhere. While I wished I could simply get the truth from her, I knew better than to push it now. She'd learn. She'd know not to lie to me. And if it was a fucking little accident, some server crashing into her, he'd be fired.

Killed, even.

I wouldn't ever apologize to avenge the slightest wrong on her behalf.

"Let's go." I took her hand, glad that she didn't shy away from my touch or try to cower from me. She gripped my fingers and held on tightly, almost as though she needed the security of my touch.

Dammit. I wish we never came. Staying at home, with her, was always the better option.

We exited the ballroom, but before we reached the car in the lot, a pair of men approached.

"Not now. For fuck's sake, *never*. Peter, fuck off."

The Boyle didn't listen. He blocked my exit. His buddy, that same imbecile who'd accused my fighters of cheating, stood next to him and further prevented me and Cara from leaving. Any second now, my men would follow. I'd tasked Ian to speak with him, but someone was always behind me, never that far on my tail. That was simply part of being a leader. I was seldom caught alone.

"I won't fuck off," Peter argued. "I heard a little interesting story recently. Something about your trying to claim a right to my family's wealth."

I scowled, keeping Cara close. "What the fuck would I want with your dirty money? The Sullivans have always had more than you could ever dream of."

"Riches and bitches, huh?" his friend joked, looking at Cara.

"Shut up," she sneered.

"Yeah," Peter said, puffing up his chest like he was some kind of a badass. "I was told you were trying to help yourself to a taste of our name, our influence, marrying someone related to a Boyle."

. . .

"What?" Cara's confusion leaked out with her one-word question. She looked from me to him, and with that distraction, I wasn't quick enough to pull my gun out before Peter held up his.

"Shut the fuck up," I said as I lifted my gun from its holster. "That's nothing but a goddamn rumor."

"I thought so at first too," the second man said.

I cocked my gun and aimed it at him. He was only asking for it, pointing his at me. "Yeah, and where'd you hear that? Who told you that rumor?" I demanded. Dad had told me that Keira started up that falsehood, but speaking with another friend tonight, when I was pulled aside that one and only time when Cara somehow got hurt, I learned that it wasn't her.

"Shane Murray?" I guessed, filling it in for him.

Peter nodded, not lowering his gun.

"Yeah," the other man said. "Murray." He smiled at Cara. "Your daddy." As he reached out to touch her arm, she batted his hand away.

"Don't touch me," she warned, angling closer to me.

I thrust my gun at him.

"Found yourself a feisty one, eh?" he taunted.

"Hold on. Hold on." Peter swatted at his buddy, shutting him up. "Why'd Shane make up that shit in the first place?"

"Because he owes me a lot of money. He owes Donal Sullivan a lot of money. It seems that he still doesn't want to pay up."

The crony laughed. "What, you take his daughter *and* wanna come for his money too?"

Peter grimaced, elbowing him. "Shut up."

"Murray owed my father before my wife was even born. His debts go way back, and yes, I'm going to fucking collect on it."

Peter seemed unconvinced. "Then why would he make up shit about your wife being related to a Boyle?"

"I'm not," Cara insisted, still clueless to what was going on.

"Through your whore of a mother," the other man said. "Rumor was that your whoring mama was related to a Boyle."

"Don't call her a whore!"

I held Cara back, annoyed that she'd try to charge at them when they held up guns.

"So, let me guess," Peter drawled, enjoying this way too much. "He started shit about your trying to trespass into the Boyle family in the hopes that what, I'd kill you and he wouldn't have to pay up?"

That's exactly what I think happened.

"I mean..." Peter smirked. "I'd never turn down a chance to remove a piece of shit like you from the face of the earth."

"Fuck you," I warned. "Let us pass before my men get ahold of you."

"Now why the fuck should I do that?" Peter set his gun down on a ledge built into the brick wall. "When it would be so much more fun to see if the infamous Declan Sullivan is worth half the fighter that he claims to be?"

I ground my molars together, knowing exactly what he was doing.

Challenging me.

Trying to have a little entertainment, pissing me off.

Goading me into a fight just to prove a stupid point.

I'd fought him before, and it seemed he was overdue a reminder of how badly I'd beaten him last time.

"Stand back." I handed Cara my gun, not trusting this second Boyle not to grab it.

Where the fuck is Ian? I didn't need backup. Not for myself. I could take this ugly asshole down, both of them. But I had to make sure Cara was safe. I didn't want to tell her to run to the ballroom. She was safest with me. No one would defend her as much as I would.

My hands were tied, and it seemed like she wasn't an amateur at holding the gun, anyway. She lifted my handgun with both hands, shaking, but with a proper grip.

"You're going to regret this," I warned him as I braced myself to fight. Flicking my fingers, I gestured for him to take his best shot and come at me.

"No, I won't." He smirked, walking in a slight circle, calculating his approach. "You're gonna regret showing your wife what a weak-ass pussy you are—"

I slammed my fist into his face. Just like that, it was on.

He wasn't as bad as I thought he would be, but that was okay. I hadn't lowered my guard and I wouldn't. His form was shit, but he packed power in the hits he could manage to land on me.

Time blurred. The suspense and adrenaline rush of violence filled me, and I didn't know whether we fought for seconds or minutes.

My knuckles bled. He was missing a tooth. Both of our bodies would bear the evidence of a hard battle. We punched and kicked, jabbed and dropped each other to the pavement. All throughout the scrimmage, I tried my best to keep himself between him and Cara, to maintain her position at my back so I could not only teach this Boyle asshole a lesson about taunting me into a fight, but also so I could protect her from that other man who'd stepped back to let his buddy handle this unnecessary challenge.

"I wouldn't be surprised if you did try to marry into our family," Peter taunted. He grinned, his teeth so bloody that he looked maniacal. "Because you're nothing but scum. Never will be anything more than a waste of space."

I growled, sick of his stupidity. I didn't give a shit about his family. I didn't want to be aligned with my enemy. They could all rot in hell, but Peter's teasing rubbed me too far the wrong way.

"I wouldn't stoop to making up a fucking rumor about my wife's family." I glanced at her, not liking how close that other man came toward her. She held the gun up, but her worried focus was on me.

Peter grunted, landing a hard hook on my chin while I was distracted. "Like hell you wouldn't."

"Are you suggesting that I'm a liar?" I was sick of lies. Of people lying to me. Of wondering who else would try to deceive me.

I lunged quicker than he could have counted on. Wrapping my arms around him, I knocked him to the ground and locked his head against me. My biceps shook. My elbow strained. And with Peter stuck in a chokehold, I grabbed my fist to deepen the noose of my arm over his neck.

To the death, motherfucker.

Just as he struggled, trying and failing with that panicked frenzy of knowing his life was almost over, a gunshot went off. Then another. Cara screamed. And another gun was fired.

A searing slice of fire bit into my arm, and it was all that other man needed to dissuade me from killing Peter. I groaned, wincing at the graze, and struggled to keep Peter in the chokehold.

"Cara!" I stared at her, worried she'd been hit. She had to have fired at least once.

Peter escaped my grip, and I hurried toward Cara to get my gun back.

By the time I reached her, Peter reclaimed his gun.

"Fuck you, De—"

I spun, taking the bullet he'd aimed at her. It streaked against my arm, cutting my flesh where I'd already been hit.

Shoving Cara had saved her. I pushed her out of the way just in time, and as I completed my pivot, I fired at both men. Fast.

They fell, dead, bullets into their brains from the clean shot between their eyes.

I heaved out a deep breath as the sound of hurried footsteps sounded closer.

"Declan?" Ian called out.

Cara whimpered, reaching out for me.

I exhaled a long breath again, looking down at her terrified and stunned on the pavement.

Then with another blink, I felt dizzy, exhausted from bleeding so quickly.

"Are you okay?"

She scrambled to stand. "Am *I* okay?" Her arms rose. With a shaky first step, she reached out to me, and I leaned against her embrace.

24

CARA

My heart thumped so wildly, I thought it would never slow down. My throat strained as I tried to swallow, but it was thick, clogged with so many intense emotions.

Terror. Anger. And so, so much worry.

Declan sighed and leaned against me, and his weight comforted me.

He stood. He was breathing. He lived.

But the consuming fear of almost losing him would take a lot longer to subside.

"Are you…?" I couldn't dare to ask him if he was all right. He couldn't possibly be. He'd fought so hard, beaten and tired from the strain of it. Then he was shot, at least once. He lived, but until I knew how wounded he was, I wouldn't be calm.

I'd never been this close to violence before. I'd never aimed a weapon at a person. Although I was braced for combat with many experiences with wild or unruly animals, it was not at all the same as being near men with guns and a desire to fight.

"No." Declan winced as he stepped back to better look me over. Ian ran closer, and other men hurried with him.

"No?" I swallowed hard, worried even more now that Declan could admit that he was hurt.

"No, don't worry about me. Are *you* okay?" He lowered his worried gaze to my stomach. "Did I hurt you in that fall?"

Realization sank in. He was concerned about my body. If I could've landed on my stomach.

If I could hurt the baby he's so desperately hoping I carry.

It stung. I wanted to matter too. Just me. And that guilt rose up again, inciting shame within my mind.

There won't be a baby.

"I'm fine."

"Let's go," Ian said, not even checking whether his brother was all right. I supposed in their world, in their code, if a man was standing, breathing, and speaking, he would make it.

Sullivan guards checked the bodies on the ground, but I barely glanced at them as Declan ushered me into the parking lot.

"Declan." I shook my head, unable to loosen this grip of anxiety.

If I lost him. If he was hurt and killed...

"It's over," he said simply as Ian covered our backs, rushing us into the first SUV that pulled up.

Last night, Declan had wanted to leave and spend the night here, in the city, closer to the ballroom. My request for him to help me choose a gown turned into being another hour late. Then another. So much so that we fucked all night at home, at the castle, and only came to this gala just before it started.

The plan was to stay in the city tonight, but I was relieved that the driver checked that he was driving to the family home. The castle. For almost a month, I was so sick of being imprisoned there. Since Declan and I had come to terms and found our way toward each other with hot sex, it was a place of refuge, of security that I could share with him.

I was glad we were going there, and in the backseat, I tried to stay out of the way but also help as Ian handed him gauze from the front seat.

"Here." I yanked on Declan's sleeve when he struggled to get it off. The fabric ripped, but I didn't care.

"Get the shirt, too," Ian ordered.

I nodded. I'd helped plenty of sheep and horses. Declan was a man, but it couldn't be that different. As the vehicle sped along, Ian handed me gauze to compress the wounds.

"You're not afraid of blood, are you?" he asked.

I glanced at Declan, worried when he hissed at the last stretch to get his shirt off. I helped, ripping it and removing it at last.

"No. Give me that water bottle," I instructed. "I need to irrigate the wound."

"What, are you a fucking doctor, too?" Declan joked, clenching his teeth as I squirted the water on the cuts.

"No." At the thought of a doctor, I thought back to all the ones Mom had to see. All the ones who'd tried to keep her comfortably alive for so long. And the private privileges for advanced, faster medical care that I was behind on debt-wise.

Together, with Ian handing me first-aid supplies from the front, we aided Declan on the ride home. I wrapped his arm, glad that it looked like grazes more than anything. His flesh was torn up. The tattoos that had been inked there were now destroyed, but I saw nothing like muscles exposed. They were deep enough to cause pain if the grimaces lining his face were any indication, but they seemed shallow enough that a simple line of stitches would cure him.

Stitches I wasn't confident to give him on the road, even if supplies were on hand.

"He'll be waiting for us when we pull up," Ian told Declan, explaining that he'd called ahead to the house and requested a family doctor to be on hand.

Lucky. Private, family doctors. It felt so wrong to feel this way, but I couldn't help but think back to my stepmother's taunt, that if I wanted money for my mom, I could ask my wealthy husband.

I never should've had to consider that option. My father was supposed to cover it. And I couldn't know yet whether Declan would use my mother's illnesses against me.

He couldn't. I didn't want to think that he could still be so cruel. I saw the worry on his face when he stood. He'd taken a bullet for me and pushed me to safety. That mattered. It had to matter more than anything and serve as a real example of how much he was coming to care for me.

Maybe he could care so much that he wouldn't want to hurt me.

"Tell me what happened," Declan said, taking my hand as we rode home. "When I fought Peter."

I licked my lips and explained it all to both brothers. How the other man had tried to creep closer to me, but I'd warned him off with the gun.

Declan frowned. "Have you ever used a gun before?"

I nodded, then shook my head.

"Which is it?" Ian asked.

"I've used a gun on wild animals, but not on a person." They seemed satisfied with that, so I continued. "When you tried to…" I winced.

"Choke that first guy, the other one shot at you. So I fired at him, but missed. Then he shot again but missed."

I'd never been so damn scared in my life. Not only that I could die, but that I couldn't help Declan. And if I died, my mother would be screwed and I'd fail her too.

I sucked in a deep breath, so glad that we were pulling up to the castle.

Clinging to Declan, I followed him inside. To my surprise, he peeled away and stepped aside, heading for the doctor.

"I can help," I offered.

He shook his head, sighing. "Just go to bed. I'll check with you."

I furrowed my brow, worried that I'd disappointed him.

Because I lied? I'd struggled to face him after I made up that answer about a server smacking into my face, but I had no other option.

I couldn't tell him that Keira slapped me because he would have wanted to know what I talked to her about. And if I told him about my mother's debts…

My stomach knotted. A familiar nausea returned. It had been creeping up on me on and off over the last couple of days, and I wondered if it was a reaction to the constant sex. My periods had never been really regular, courtesy of those issues long ago, and I wondered if I was going through another round of PMS too soon.

Right now, I felt sick with worry. About lying to Declan. About not telling him about my mother. I just didn't know what to do, and it was with a heavy heart that I watched him head into the kitchen with the doctor.

"You're okay?" Ian asked me as I moved into the main lounge to slump to the couch. I should've gone upstairs, but I wanted to be here, close, to walk up with my husband. The doctor would help him. Declan seemed fine, but still, I worried. It had taken a few years off my life to see him fighting and shot.

There's no doubt. I cared for him. Greatly.

I glanced up at my brother-in-law. "Yeah. I…" I sighed. "I'm fine."

When he didn't leave, I wondered why he lingered. He seemed suspicious, and I felt guarded, on the need to be defensive. "What is it?"

I hadn't talked with Ian much, but that didn't count for anything. Other than that one or two chats with Riley, I spoke with only Declan here.

"I'm aware of how you ran at the wedding."

I groaned, dropping my head to the back of the couch. "That was the *only* time."

"So, I shouldn't worry about your trying to run off when Dec's vulnerable and wounded?"

I stood, annoyed. "Vulnerable?" I crossed my arms and glared at him. "Have you *ever* seen him vulnerable?"

He almost smiled.

"I'm not going to run," I promised as I walked past him and headed upstairs.

It was the truth. I couldn't escape here, and I had no desire to break away from the man I called my husband. How could I want to leave when he made me feel so free, so cared for and cherished?

That fight in the parking area seemed so brutal and awful, but I hadn't viewed Declan as anything but a hero. A valiant, strong protector. Not a villain. Not a "bad guy" like my stepsister seemed to think of him.

Declan was rough and gruff. But I'd seen the sweetness and tenderness he hid beneath the darkness to know he wasn't all bad.

I wanted to stay with him. As I walked up the stairs, wondering if he'd see me in my room again, I vowed to come clean.

About it all.

The reason I was scared of him upon first sight. The deal that I'd made with my father to take my stepsister's place and be the bride. Why I was afraid to tell him.

Everything.

Even the worse secret about my infertility. He had every right to know that I couldn't bear him a child, and I felt sicker with anxiety to keep that from him.

All of it. I had to tell him everything.

If I could admit how much I wanted to stay and truly be his wife, for good, he had to know it all.

It was only fair. Shame ate at me as I opened my door and then closed it behind me. I felt terrible, guilty and wretched the longer I kept the secret from him.

Resting my head against the closed door, I dropped my shoulders and just breathed through the heartache of knowing I'd wronged him in not being upfront.

My phone rang, pulling me from my trancelike mood of worry and gloom.

I frowned, reaching for my phone on the nightstand. I hadn't considered bringing it. Why should I? Oscar and my mother wouldn't contact me. They'd wait for me to reach out with the spotty reception they thought I had.

But it wasn't either of them. The number on the screen seemed vaguely familiar, but I couldn't place it.

"Hello?" I answered, glancing at the door. I was worried about who it could be. Declan wanted me to use this only to speak with my mother, and I knew he'd be mad and see this as breaking the rules.

"Cara Gallagher?" the woman asked.

"Yes."

"I'm calling from the hospital. You are listed as the sole emergency contact for your mother. Nora Gallagher? Yes, that's it. She's just arrived at the Emergency Department."

I sucked in a quick breath and held it.

Once more, I felt my world tipping off its axis.

And the sensation of everything falling apart threatened to suffocate me all over again for the second time tonight.

25

DECLAN

Ian walked into the kitchen just as the doctor finished sewing me up. Riley slid him a glass of whiskey, and I held my empty one up for her to take.

"Frank's here," my brother announced.

I glanced from my new stitches to the guard entering the room. He was at the gala with us, still one of Cara's primary guards, so I wondered why he seemed to just be getting here.

"He stayed to help clean up," Ian said as Frank slumped to a stool at the island.

"I'm going to check on your father, and I'll be off," the doctor said, taking his leave.

"Thank you." I turned to Frank, willing to give him two seconds of my attention before going to my wife. I didn't care if she swore she wasn't hurt. I saw that she had been. Maybe not from my shove to protect her, but by someone's hand in the moment I'd left her alone.

"I was also one of the men near Cara when she slipped away at the gala," Frank said.

"Slipped away?" I didn't like the wording of that. I'd asked Ian to stick with her, but someone else had intercepted and found him. I didn't fault him. Cara could've stayed near him, but she'd left his side too.

"She sought out her stepmother," Frank said. "I saw from a distance. It was too crowded to get close quickly enough. Then her stepsister slapped her."

"Saoirse?" I knew the younger woman was a bitch, but why?

"I wasn't close enough, and another guest was blocking my view from the side, but I clearly saw Cara arguing with the stepsister, or both of them saying something heatedly, then I saw a hand connected with Cara's cheek and her head flew back. Both of the Murray women walked away, but by the time I caught up to her, you'd found her."

"Thank you." This strange sensation of being in the dark had to stop now. I stood and left them all, heading straight to Cara's room.

And found her in tears.

All this time, I wondered if she was so hardy, so tough on the outside, to be capable of crying. I had my proof.

"Cara?" I closed the doors behind me and hurried to sit next to her on the bed. "What is it?"

She sniffled and wiped her cheeks, so defeated that she didn't have any fight left in her. No flinch at my presence. No smirk or smart remark to bicker with me like usual.

Instead, she faced me and killed me with her glossy, sad eyes. "The hospital called. My mother's been taken to the emergency room."

I didn't move, caught in the memories of all the times Ian and I had been in and out of the emergency room for Dad. It never felt good, and the worry about a parent was no small thing. "I'm sorry to hear that." I was, and I hoped to back up my words with a hand on hers. Her skin felt so cool to the touch, and I wondered if she was going into shock or something.

"Has she been ill? Or…" I felt stupid and unprepared. I knew nothing about her mother other than her past, that she wasn't a Boyle.

"For years." She sat up straighter even though she seemed so overwhelmed. "She's suffered an autoimmune disease, cancer on and off, an infection… the list is long."

Fuck. That sounded like a lot.

"And now she's at the hospital. I obviously can't go to see her because I'm here. Then the privatized doctor who's been most helpful with her isn't cooperating because I'm behind on all the bills." She grimaced, pressing her free hand into a fist and shoving it into the mattress.

"What?" I stared at her, stunned. This was a lot to take in, but that didn't sound right. Behind on bills? What bills? She lived here, and her mother surely had her own income at home.

She lowered her head but brought it right back up. "I'm sorry, Declan. I'm so sorry I wasn't honest."

I braced myself for a brutal hit of truth. I should've been happy that she was owning up to her dishonesty, but I loathed being manipulated or lied to.

"I agreed to marry you because my father said he'd do me a 'favor' if I did. He and Keira didn't want Saoirse to marry you, so they used me. They'd never acknowledged me other than that one time my mother demanded he cover my hospital bill in the city. Otherwise, we didn't contact each other. They'd erased me from their lives, but when it came time to preventing their *beloved* daughter from being married to you, I was a convenient backup."

I'd wondered. "What was the favor?"

"He said that he would cover all of my mother's outstanding debt. All the medical costs and bills. Everything. He also agreed to fund her placement on the list for a kidney transplant. If she doesn't have that surgery, she will suffer for years, chronically."

Anger started on a slow simmer, but now it heated up faster. The need to hurt that spineless man was almost too much to bear. "At the church." I narrowed my eyes as I recalled the moment Cara had paled and so quickly agreed to stand at the altar with me. "What did you receive on your phone that made you change your mind?"

She wiped her cheeks. "I hadn't really changed my mind. In exchange for my mother's health and to not be drowning in debt, I agreed to marry you before I had any idea who you were. When I saw you, I was scared. You looked so angry and impatient, and I had a knee-jerk reaction. Fight or flight. And I ran, but I reminded myself what was at stake."

I gritted my teeth. "What did you see on your phone, then?" I demanded.

"Keira texted me. She'd gotten a copy of a document about Mom being on that replacement waitlist, and she threatened to pay to have Mom taken off it if I didn't go along with their deal."

I stiffened. "That was the deal you mentioned that time."

She nodded as another tear streaked over her smooth cheek. "It was. I'm sorry I didn't explain."

I couldn't be mad at her. She'd done the same thing I had. I'd forced Shane to give me his daughter in exchange for clearing his debt, only I'd changed my mind after the fact.

Shit. Did he do the same thing to her?

"Let me guess." I thought back to her words. That she was behind on bills. "He didn't pay, did he?"

She shook her head. "When you gave me my phone yesterday, I called home, and the stable hand who's more like an uncle, like family, mentioned something that didn't add up. So, I logged online and saw that everything was still owed. You walked in when I was about to call my father and ask what was going on, but then I planned to ask him in person at the gala."

I shook my head. "But you approached Keira instead?"

She winced slightly. "No. I couldn't find my father. She found me and laughed in my face when I asked about the debt being paid. She said that they never clarified *when* they'd pay it off, and she implied that they wouldn't."

You're a dead man, Murray.

"Why did your stepsister slap you?" I asked, looking at her cheek again. "That's what Frank saw."

She sighed and lowered her gaze. "No. Keira did."

I clenched my teeth and breathed through the rush of fury escalating within me even more.

"All my life, I've been working and trying to stay afloat. When they asked me to do something for them in order to cover Mom's issues, I jumped on it. I had to. I have been so exhausted for years, thinking there would never be a way out of that life, nothing to look forward to but work and the worry that I wouldn't be able to secure her spot on that organ transplant list."

I sighed, hanging my head. "Why didn't you tell me?"

She huffed a weak, teary laugh. "When? When you fucked me and left? When I thought you meant it that I didn't matter as anything but a woman to give you a baby, an heir?"

That was my own fault. I couldn't deny it. Before I got to know her at all, that was exactly how I'd treated her, too cautious that she wouldn't last.

Now, though...

"And I can't even do that." She covered her face, burying it behind her hands as she cried softly again.

"What?" The sound of her tears tore at me, but I couldn't reach out and comfort her until I understood. *Can't what?*

"I can't give you anything. I can't give you an heir."

I narrowed my eyes. No. That couldn't be possible. Ian vetted her after the fact. The Sullivans' private doctor would have noticed it on her record and told me.

If he had all *the records.*

"What are you saying?"

She lifted her face, blinking through her tears. "I can't have a baby. I had complications with a ruptured ovarian cyst when I was a teen. They removed one ovary, and the other was damaged. I'm infertile."

I stood, glaring down at her. She'd kept this all from me.

"You..."

She suggested that she stay my wife for six months unless she was pregnant, knowing damn well that she wouldn't be.

"You can't have kids?" I had to hear her repeat it so this new bombshell of truth could sink in.

She shook her head. "I'm sorry. I'm so sorry I kept it from you. But I had to secure a way out. To look out for myself but still go through with what my father expected of me in order to get Mom taken care of."

I paced away from the bed, whirling back to glare at her. Rage took over. Confusion swarmed within me too.

"You're telling me..." I growled, unable to accept this.

"I'm sorry. I was just trying to do the best I could. And I still am. I'm trying my best to do the right thing."

"The right thing is *not* fucking lying to me."

She furrowed her brow, getting some of that sass back. "Oh, so when you told me you didn't want to suffer through having a wife, just to get an heir, I was supposed to pipe up and say, nope, look around for someone else because I can't do that? Then I never would have gotten Mom taken care of—or so I thought at the time."

I stared her down, mesmerized by the fight that never died in her emerald gaze. No matter what. She'd stand up and fight until the end of any cause she set herself to.

"Are you telling me that it is impossible for you to have a child?"

I had to know. After all, that was the reason I'd married her in the first place!

Her slender shoulders lifted and fell. "I don't remember all that the doctors told me. Mom wasn't there, back at the farm to deal with an issue. I heard the doctors, and I was groggy and so confused, but the discharge papers listed it all. That I'd lost so much and wouldn't be likely to have children. I grew up assuming I never would."

"It was cruel to let me think you could." I shook my head, walking away. Cruel, but I could understand her motives.

And now that we'd gotten close… I knew my reasons for having her in my life had changed.

I wanted her to be my wife because of something that I suspected was profound love.

I loved her, and knowing she'd been so scared she'd stayed strong and hidden her woes from me suggested that she'd never return that affection.

"Cara, answer me plainly. Can you have children?"

She chewed on her lip, lowering her gaze again. "I don't know, Declan. I'm unable to tell you that. I can't predict the future. All I can explain—too late to expect forgiveness—is that I likely never will."

Likely isn't set in stone.

A stubborn, almost zealous hope took seed in my mind.

If there were any possible chance she could…

I wouldn't compromise that. She was my wife. And she would be my last.

Twisted up with her news, I stormed out of her room, unsure how to react without worsening the situation. Foremost in my thoughts was that she'd duped me, and that was a sentiment I wanted to shed right now.

I was supposed to be the one in control, always.

I'd never felt further from it as I hurried away from her soulful, sad eyes and soft, heart-wrenching sobs.

26

CARA

I couldn't blame Declan for storming out of my room.

It was the worst-case scenario I'd feared. His face registered pure shock. All that confusion that shone in his eyes made me feel even worse, like he struggled to understand how or why I'd deceived him at all.

We started our marriage based on lies. We met each other under the force of manipulation. And still to this day, we were bound to our own selfish wishes.

I needed to secure a better life for my mother.

He had to produce an heir.

But it seemed our best-laid plans to accomplish that were not feasible with our staying together.

After he left my room without a word, I ran to the bathroom to shower. This gown was a mockery, and I couldn't wait to get it off.

I had no business pretending to be his wife, to stand by his side and try to act like one of those fancy Mob wives, those elegant women who stood with their men like the puppets they were.

This wasn't me. I would not let myself be some idiot, dolled up in this gorgeous gown when I should be back home, toiling away on the farm and helping Mom with her care and getting her to her appointments.

"I'm such a fucking idiot," I groaned to myself as I stepped in the shower.

All this time I'd wasted. I was a fool to ever actually think there could be an easy way out of a hard life. That making a deal with my father would ever end well. That trying to sweep all my stress away in one fell swoop would really work.

Now I'd lose *him*, too. I'd told Declan that I'd give him six months. Only five remained now, and I wouldn't be any more likely to get pregnant within them. He'd leave me, per the deal we shook on at the church. He'd let me go, like he said, and I knew I would never see him again.

After the hardships that pushed me to reach him, to discover that dark, deep love that I knew couldn't be a lie, I had to lose it all with him.

I stood in the shower, letting the hot water pummel my flesh. It was a weak attempt to invigorate myself. Unless the water could seep under my skin and rinse out the guilt, shame, and building heartbreak, I would remain broken and dirty.

After I turned numb and my skin pinkened with the blast of heat, I shut the water off and got dressed to try to do damage control again.

Declan had given me my phone to call my mother only, but that rule no longer mattered to me.

If I couldn't go to her, I'd do the best I could from a distance. I called the hospital. I tried to get ahold of *all* the doctors who made up the care team for her problems. It was late, though, and I struggled to speak with anyone who could help me.

That night, I curled up on the bed holding my phone in case someone would call. I was prohibited from checking in with Mom directly. She couldn't take calls, and Oscar's phone wasn't connecting. I prayed that he, or the neighbor, was with her so that she wasn't alone, but I doubted she would understand why I wasn't at her side. She wasn't likely to forgive me for my absence, either.

With my heart breaking and my mind a ragged mess, I fell into a fitful sleep only to wake late.

Groggy and disoriented, I sat up and immediately tried all the numbers again. Faced with the same issues, I clenched my teeth and growled through the frustration of being so useless. Since it was the weekend, no offices were staffed. No one answered the phone. And the two people I did speak with weren't any help. One woman at the hospital confirmed that my mother was still in critical care, and the other person, a young man who was an after-hours receptionist at her primary doctor's office, suggested nothing more than making an appointment for three months from now for a follow-up.

I paced, so mad that the ache and tension in my stomach worsened further. Rubbing my abdomen hardly helped, and it took all my energy to breathe through the panic attack of my life coming apart.

Declan hated me.

Mom was ill.

All the debts remained.

And I was a liar, deceiving my husband. That stung the worst of all.

When my phone rang again, I answered quickly, so relieved to be able to speak with Oscar.

"Is she okay?" I asked as a greeting.

"I don't know!" The sounds of chaos filled in from his end. Machinery. Men arguing. Animals protesting. "The tractor engine caught on fire. I've been trying to salvage the farm. The buildings are damaged."

I pressed my hand to my mouth just as knocks sounded on the door. Declan wouldn't knock. The only other person here who'd seek me out would be Riley.

Tears welled in my eyes as I opened the door to let her in. "Are the animals…?"

Oscar sighed. "They're fine. Scared but fine. I've got some neighbors helping to relocate them and contain it all, but I'm sorry, Cara. I can't check on Nora."

I sniffed as Riley entered my room, eyes wide as she closed the door after her. In her hand, she held a tray of food with a cup of coffee. Breakfast. I'd missed it, but the scents of it all bothered my stomach more.

"Okay. I understand."

"It's not looking good, kid." Oscar grunted. "None of this is. I know you said you can't tell me anything about why you ran off. Hell, I wouldn't blame you. This is no life. All these worries and everything. The farm, the money, the debt, your mom. But this is the *worst* timing."

I nodded. He was wrong. I hadn't *run* off. I'd taken the first dumb idea to solve all my problems. And it had colossally backfired.

I disconnected with him when he said he had to go, and I felt worse to keep him on the phone at all, bothering him when he was trying his best.

Riley set the tray on a table, but I shook my head. "No. Please, get that out of here."

"Not feeling good?" she guessed.

I shook my head. How could I feel all right when my life was breaking apart? When my mom was suffering and my husband hated me?

"I can't do anything right," I groaned as I slumped to the couch and rubbed my stomach.

"Eh. I doubt that. I saw you make Declan smile the other day. That's a miracle in itself."

It'd be the last one, too. "He won't be so happy anymore."

"Why? What happened?" She sat on a chair across from me, seeming sincerely worried.

"Oh, God."

As she came closer, the smell of the greasy bacon wafted closer. "I'm going to puke." Covering my mouth with my hand, I tried to stave off the worst of the nausea.

"Damn. You are worrying yourself sick." She pressed her lips together in a sympathetic frown. "I bet it was scary seeing Declan hurt last night. But that's life. They're rough men, but he'll be fine. Don't let yourself dwell on the what-ifs of it all."

I shook my head. "No, it's not that." I had been worried when he was hurt, but I'd already seen for myself last night that he was fine and stitched up.

"Then what's wrong?"

I grimaced, battling the agony of my empty, upset stomach. "The smell of that bacon. And the thought of even eating. It's making the stress even worse."

She perked up, grinning. "Cara!"

I reared back at her outburst. "What?"

"You—" She stood and folded her hands together, so excited that she practically jumped.

"*What?*" I repeated.

"Are you pregnant?"

I opened and closed my mouth, trying to hurry and connect the dots. Why she'd ever leap to that conclusion was beyond me, but as I thought back to health class in high school, I realized that maybe what I was suffering could sound like morning sickness.

I'm not. I shook my head. "No. It's not that."

"You know?" She smiled. "Have you taken a test?"

I shook my head again. *Not necessary.*

"Are you late?"

I was. I thought I was. My cycles were never that consistent. I used to assume it was because I did too much manual labor and was so fit that my body never went through it. Athletes often had wonky schedules with their physique like that. And then all the stress... I never considered the details of my unreliable menstrual cycles because of my life and the complications when I was a teenager.

"No."

She tilted her head to the side. "You hesitated to answer. Are you?"

I furrowed my brow. "I'm not pregnant."

She huffed. "I know there's got to be tests in the bathroom. Try one. You might not know."

She just didn't get it. But I didn't want to lose the one friendly person here. If I had to stay married for five more months while Declan hated me, it would be hell.

Riley left me, taking the tray with her, but once she was gone, I couldn't stop thinking about what she'd said. About how my husband might treat me now that he knew I couldn't serve a purpose for him.

"Oh, for fuck's sake," I mumbled as I went to the bathroom to find the stick. I may as well prove her wrong. Declan would want the proof too.

I was sick to my stomach with stress, and as I peed on the stick, I rolled my eyes and wondered why I was bothering.

I left the test in the bathroom to fetch my glass of ice water that I did ask Riley to leave with me, and by the time a minute had passed, I returned to the bathroom to check on the package for how long this test would require to show I was infertile.

Or not.

I blinked, looking from the package to the stick.

Three more minutes remained, but two lines showed clearly already. A pair of parallel streaks darkened, and I gaped at the evidence.

Pregnant.

"Oh, my God…" I grabbed the stick and stared at it like it was a joke. I shook it. I peered at it closely, questioning the lighting of the room.

"It's got to be a fluke." I fumbled for another test, dumping out three from the box. My heart raced as I used them all, having a thread of common sense to use a cup to collect the sample in and test again. And again. And again.

I read through every single word of the fine print with the instructions. I pored over the list of steps. It didn't matter.

Every stick showed positive.

I *was* pregnant. The impossible had happened.

The doctors must have been wrong. I wasn't infertile.

I was *pregnant*.

Shock rendered me numb, but a deeper, stronger sense of excitement filled me to the point that I almost cried. Laughing instead, hysterical, I curled up on the bed and pressed my hand to my flat stomach.

"How?" I whispered, overjoyed with the fact that I would be a mother.

How in the hell?

This was a twist I couldn't have ever expected after the ups and downs of the last day. But I wasn't mad or scared about it.

I'd never wanted a child before, when I thought I couldn't have one. I formed my opinions long ago that I didn't want to ever bring a child into a poor quality of life at the farm with my hopeless circumstances. Now, with Declan in the picture, though, I was excited to share a baby with him.

Elation coursed through me as I imagined the surprise and shock that would show on his face. He would be a good father, the authoritarian, for sure, but he would provide for this child in a way I never could have dreamed of before.

But he didn't know. For the next two days, he stayed away, and I was torn apart with his absence.

I yearned to tell him how sorry I was. I wanted to express my remorse for not being honest and telling him from the beginning that I was infertile when it was no longer an issue with the new life growing inside me.

Minutes turned to hours. Hours turned to days. For two long ones, I gave in to the feeling of being out of control. Nothing was in my control anymore, and I wished so badly that I could put an end to this stress about making everything right.

The only time I ever felt so free and released from stress was when he was here. When he was fucking me hard and pushing me to pleasure, preventing me from obsessing and trying to stay in control of everything.

Now, with him seeming to block my texts and calls, with him avoiding me completely and staying away, it looked like I would be wife number three to be removed from the Sullivan estate.

27

DECLAN

Sleep was impossible, but I waited until the next day to go to see Cara's family.

Calling Shane and Keira Murray her family felt like a reach. They weren't *family* in the sense that I was with my dad and Ian. With all the men and women affiliated with the Sullivan name.

Family didn't force others to make sacrifices so they could skirt away from having to own up to their own debts. Family didn't promise to erase financial woes and then fail to come through.

Anger and rage mixed in an ugly storm, but I tamped it down and bided my time to visit the Murrays the next day.

They had been at the gala, and I didn't want to return there after Peter Boyle challenged me in the parking lot and forced me to kill him. That shit happened all the time. This was the way of the Mob life. I wouldn't be in trouble, not with the law. We carved our own rules and laws, anyway.

Still, I didn't welcome the stress of having to locate Shane Murray among the crowd that had likely already dispersed from the party by the time Cara came clean about what she was hiding.

So, with Ian on speakerphone, I drove to the Murray residence the next afternoon.

I swore I'd never set foot there again after the last time I came here with Ian, and I really hoped *this* time would be the final and very last occasion I'd ever have to face him.

"I'm on it," Ian promised, confirming that he would help me sort out this mess. I would never forget the sight of Cara's tear-streaked face last night, and I would never get past the utter devastation she suffered from.

Coming here to speak with the Murrays was the first step of this retaliation. And it wouldn't be pretty.

I was furious with Cara. It would take me a long time to move on from her lies and manipulation.

But I still cared. I couldn't hate her for what she'd done. In another sense, I had to… admire her for it. Late last night, I realized that she really had done the best she could. To secure her future and care for her mother, she'd taken the best option possible.

If I had been her position, I knew I would have done the same damn thing.

In that sense, we weren't so different. And it oddly served as a reminder that we belonged together.

I pounded my fist on the door, daring that crusty old butler to take his time letting me in. Standing at the front door, I waited and wished my brother were here. I could handle this myself, but if I got carried away, if I let my anger get the better of me, he'd be able to pull me back.

Shane and Keira Murray were about to be put in their places—for good. Ian simply had too many other things to do for me to be here to see it.

When the butler opened the door, he blanched and almost tripped on his feet in his haste to back up.

"Murray!" I bellowed, running into the foyer and searching the fancy décor. It was gaudy, every bit of it, and I knew they'd be saying goodbye to it all very soon.

No one approached, and I didn't bother waiting for the butler to call for them or to announce that they had a visitor. With the dark mood I was in, I was no *visitor*. I was an executioner. A deliverer of bad news.

I found them in the kitchen, catching the husband and wife in the middle of what seemed to be a heated argument. Keira shut up at once, scowling at my presence as she pushed Shane in front of her. She no doubt recalled how I'd handled my last conversation with her.

Knowing she'd slapped Cara pushed me to nearly losing my temper, but she wasn't worth a hit in return. The message I had to share with her would be the ultimate punishment for a selfish, shallow bitch like her.

"What are you doing here?" she demanded.

I stalked forward and grabbed the front of Shane's shirt. He flinched, wrestling to get free as I slammed him into a chair at their table. When I turned to his wife, I glowered and pointed at the next one. "Sit your ugly ass down."

"This is—"

I lost my control. I lifted my hand to smack her, but I stopped. I couldn't. I wouldn't stoop to her level. I had my wits, and I knew she'd suffer more from what I was about to explain.

She crouched, bracing for the hit as she slunk to sit next to her husband. Shane reached for her hand to hold it, but she snatched it out of his reach. "Now what did you do?" she sneered, assuming I was here because of her husband's actions.

I was. But I had no clue how else he might have fucked up since he'd coerced Cara to marry me.

He was an idiot. A cheat. He owed me money. He had dues with other families, like whatever incident happened last time when Keira begged me to help him out. No one could ever help this dumbass, and I would never want to.

"Did you ever intend to cover the medical debts for Nora Gallagher?" I demanded.

As soon as the words left my mouth, I felt stupid. *Of course*, he never intended to pay up for the "favor" he'd expected of his eldest daughter. Just like he never intended to pay my father back. Or anyone else.

Courtesy of what I heard at the gala, I also knew that he and/or Keira framed that rumor about my marrying into a distant, illegitimate relation of the Boyles in hopes that they'd kill me and avoid having to pay *me* back after I reneged and told them that they still owed every cent.

"What?" Shane paled. His mouth hung open. His eyes were wide with panic.

Keira reacted differently. She scowled like a bad taste wouldn't leave her mouth. "She told you?"

"Did you?" I demanded. I didn't care how cold and brutal I was. They deserved all my hatred.

Shane shook his head, slowly but then too vigorously like he couldn't stop from trembling. "No. I, uh, well, I…"

"*No*," Keira answered, clearer and firmer. She crossed her arms. "Never."

"No?" I asked her, tilting my head to the side as I considered slapping that smug expression off her face.

"No. I never want to acknowledge her at all. All this time, it's been a stain on *my* life that he had to admit she was his daughter at all."

"But you didn't hesitate to acknowledge her and use her when it was for your benefit," I said.

She nodded. "I would never let *my* daughter be with someone like you."

"Someone strong? Successful?"

That prissy huff made her even uglier. "Cara was nothing more than the daughter of a whore. Being with you is all she deserved."

I leaned forward, gripping both of their necks and squeezing them tightly. "And do you know what *you* deserve?"

Shane spluttered, clawing at his neck. Keira fidgeted, staring at me with complete loathing.

"You will pay back every penny owed to my father. To me. And from this day forward, you will never interfere with my wife's life *ever* again."

I tightened my fingers.

Shane nodded.

Keira merely pressed her lips tighter together, damned to agree.

"Killing you would be too easy. I will see to it that you suffer every minute of poverty and hardship to pay back all of your debts with revised interest." I released Shane but gripped Keira's neck tighter. "And neither of you will ever interfere in my life, in my wife's life. Ever. *Again.*"

She coughed, wheezing for air as I released her.

"Have I made myself perfectly fucking clear?" I asked as I straightened my cuffs and stepped back.

"Yes. Yes, Mr. Sullivan," Shane replied shakily.

I cast one more glowering look at Keira, then narrowed my eyes at a frightened and angry Saoirse hiding in the back of the room too.

After I left, I exhaled all my pent-up fury in the car.

I doubted my rage with the Murrays would ever dissipate. I hated how they'd let her down.

And I dreaded the thought that she might assume I was letting her down as well.

I wasn't. I had to make things right first, that was all.

Ian was checking with her medical records to see just how low her chances of pregnancy were.

If she only had half of a chance of conceiving, we would just have to try twice as hard and prepare for double the patience.

As I drove away from her worthless father's mansion that he'd need to sell soon to repay me, I knew without a doubt that Cara *would* be the mother of my children. She was the only woman I wanted to be my spouse. No one else.

Before I could return to the estate home and teach her that lesson, I had another stop to make.

Ian could handle the majority of the bills, the payments, and all that administrative crap.

It was past time that I checked in on my mother-in-law and took over the situation where she was suffering.

Because I love you, Cara, I will move heaven and earth for you.

I loved her.

Which made it hurt all the more when I had to recall that she so clearly didn't feel the same about me.

If she could still be so hesitant and hold out for so long to not tell me about her troubles, not to ask me for help or be honest with me, she couldn't feel this deep, burrowing love that I did.

And I was sobered by how badly I wanted her love in return.

28

CARA

Declan wasn't back.

Every time I looked at the doors, I wondered if this would be the moment when he'd surprise me and return. Letting my hopes get up, I clung to the wish that I would have a chance to explain and apologize again.

Missing him was a full-body effort. I felt deprived of energy, all my willpower centralized on yearning for him to just come back.

Guilt ate at me, and I hated that I'd ever tried to hide my issues and worries from him for so long.

My phone died, and when Riley gave me a charger cord, I learned that it was just dead. It was an older model, all I could afford, and with it punking out on me and preventing me from checking in with Oscar or my mom, or to keep up with my attempts to figure out what was going on at the hospital, I was stuck and helpless.

I'd never felt so out of control like this, and it was nothing similar to the freeing liberation that Declan gave me when he pushed me to my limits sexually, with his strong body so good when it fit in and against mine.

I went to bed, frustrated and so sad, and I still stared at the doors.

I wasn't sure at this rate whether my husband would ever return. It all seemed so hopeless. So ill-fated. And I hated that things could ever come apart with this sequence. That just as I learned of the miracle that I was pregnant, the father of my baby wouldn't want anything to do with me. That as I realized the depth of my feelings for him, he'd turned away and was hurt by what I'd done and said.

The doorknob clicked, and I blinked away the slight drowsiness that had come. Sitting upright in the bed, I stared, shocked and so relieved, as Declan strode inside.

He kept his dark, intense gaze on me as he paused to reach back. Once more, the metal clicked. He locked the door behind him and approached me. Like a predator honing in on his prey.

I sat up, scrambling to get out of the covers and sheets to address him. I'd waited and stressed over this confrontation, but I wouldn't shy away from making it happen now. I had so much to tell him, and he had to hear me out.

"Don't say a word," he ordered as he yanked his tie off.

I blinked, stepping back toward the bed. That sinister glint of violence in his eyes seemed so familiar, yet not. Until this moment, I hadn't realized the depth of his hatred for me. How dark and severe his loathing could grow.

"Dec—"

He reached up, gagging me with his tie. His gaze locked on mine, and in his eyes I saw every bit of command and authority he held, all that he expected me to obey.

I breathed faster through my nose, panicked and worried. He *was* in a mood, and my chances of speaking—of explaining and apologizing again—wouldn't be happening.

"On the bed," he ordered, removing his shirt and then reaching in the drawers for a silky length of fabric.

I shook, trembling as I climbed back on the bed. By the time I was lying down, staring up at him, he was after me, binding my hands to the bedframe, quickly pulling my loose nightgown off my body. I hadn't bothered with underwear, and his hungry, wicked glare remained there. Maybe I'd surprised him, but that wasn't my intention.

"I'm going to fuck you, *Wife*," he promised as he shoved his fingers in my pussy.

I arched up at the instant stretch. My gasp was choked back with the gag over my mouth. But his rushed touch wasn't completely rough. Just his look could make me aroused. Suspended between fear and desire, he found the evidence of my slippery juices.

"I'm going to pound into you so hard, and you'd better pray I'm in a better mood afterward," he growled as he smeared my cream back to my ass.

I squeezed my eyes tight. It burned. His fingers felt so big there at this hole, and as he slowly inserted them, the intense sting turned to forbidden pleasure.

"I'm going to fuck your mouth." He leaned down to suck at my tits until his lips would bruise my flesh. "I'm going to fuck this cunt." He moved to pull my clit between his teeth and flick his tongue at the bundle of nerves. "And I'm going to claim this ass." He added another finger, stretching me out as he watched me writhe and strain against the ties.

His legs straddled my right thigh, holding me down.

He'd trapped me, with bindings and his body. With the dark, twisted promise of so many filthy, rotten, but seductively perfect things he wanted to do.

I dripped for him. My pussy ached. My nipples stung. I wanted him, so damn badly, but I was too scared.

He wasn't doing this out of love or to make me happy. He was mad. He was taking his anger out on me. While I still knew he'd make me come and see to it that I was pleasured, I feared it would be too much.

Too rough.

What about the baby?

It felt like such a ridiculous worry, that if my husband took me hard and fucked me ten ways to hell, he could hurt my baby.

But what did I know? I'd never considered being pregnant, and I didn't care if I was overexaggerating my worries.

While I wasn't sure if it was smart to be this rough sexually, I got stuck on an even more potent feeling of unease.

I didn't want him to take me like this. All that he threatened sounded like heaven. I wanted him, all of him, and I wanted to give everything to him in return. But I didn't want to be a body to fuck. I didn't want to be a *thing* to him.

I wanted him to make love to me, to fuck me with that unrelenting love that I couldn't stop myself from feeling for him.

I shook my head, staring at him with tears building in my eyes. Blinking and looking at him so scared, I prayed that he'd get the message.

No.

Wait.

Please. Wait.

He scowled, getting off the bed and glaring down at me. "What?" He shook his head, walking to the bathroom and grumbling to himself as he washed his hands and came back with a washcloth and a tube of lube.

"What?" he demanded, apparently taking my muted protests as a complaint that it stung too much.

He shoved my gag down and arched his brow at me.

"Don't..." I panted, staring at him. "Don't hurt me."

He narrowed his eyes.

"Don't hurt the baby."

"What?"

I licked my lips. "Please. I'm sorry."

"*What?*"

I lost the fight on my tears. One streaked free. "I didn't feel well. When you stormed off, I was so sick with worry and stress. About you. About my mom. And when Riley brought me breakfast and said I might be suffering from morning sickness when the smell of food turned me off, I thought I'd humor her—and myself—and take a test."

He frowned, staring at me so seriously that he seemed unable to believe me. "You're pregnant?"

I nodded quickly, helpless to stop the small smile on my lips. "I took a test and I thought it was a mistake. Declan, I can't. I don't know how—I wasn't—I'm not supposed to be able to conceive. That's what I believed since I was a teenager. I didn't believe it, but I took seven more tests just to make sure."

"You're pregnant." It seemed like a question but sounded more like he was trying to convince himself that it was true.

"Yes. I'm pregnant. With your baby. I'm sorry. I'm so sorry I ever married you thinking that I would remain childless. I truly don't know how this happened."

"How else would it happen?" he shot back.

I swallowed, so nervous that he would *still* be so mad. He got off the bed and paced, running his hand through his hair.

"I'm sorry, Declan. For everything. For ever lying and trying to manipulate the situation."

I'd tell him a thousand times over if that was how long it would take for the truth to sink into his head. I would never stop professing my sorrow and regret there.

When he remained cool and pensive, not coming back to me, I reverted to that pit of dread. That feeling of being out of control and failing.

"Declan, this is what you wanted."

"It's kind of a surprise." He shook his head, looking anywhere but at me as he struggled to comprehend this news. "You *just* told me that you couldn't conceive, and now—"

"I know. No one can be more surprised than me."

Does he not believe me?

"The tests are in the bathroom. I was hoping and wishing you'd come home so I could tell you, so I could tell you first. But hopefully, I can find a doctor and have them confirm it. And I want to start prenatal care as soon as possible. Anything I can do to help this baby be healthy." Deep down, I worried about any complications that might arise. I'd been under the assumption that I had reproductive issues, and I couldn't help but be stressed that making this pregnancy a healthy and successful one would be my next challenge.

"Declan?" I licked my lips, breathless and anxious for him to reply and react in any other way than pacing and not meeting my eyes. "I know it's a shock…"

Please don't tell me I've been wrong about you. That you do care. And might love me.

He seemed so stuck in his mood, angry and surprised, that I lost all faith.

He'd gotten his heir. That was all he'd ever wanted. That was the end goal.

He no longer had to pretend that he cared about me. He no longer had to try to fuck me or resume any form of intimacy, especially the dark, rough kind that I'd come to need from him to let go.

All I was good for was giving him a baby, but I hated that *I* couldn't hold any more value to him.

"Declan…" I sniffled, hating that tears fell so easily around him now.

He stopped, facing me with his hand raised, pausing as he raked his hair back.

"What?"

I also want you to know that… I love you.

No words could come.

29

DECLAN

"What?" I turned back to her, suspended with tension for what else she might say.

This magnificent woman had given me so many ups and downs. Life was a roller coaster with her, and I wasn't sure why she would be looking at me like this, worried and anxious.

And sad.

Does she not want this baby?

"I love you," she whispered.

I froze, letting her sweet confession fill my mind and patch my heart.

"What did you say?" I stalked closer to her, impatient to hold her and look into her eyes for any hint of a lie as she repeated it.

She was still bound, and I rectified that as I reached her. Kneeling on the bed, I untied her as she stared up at me, her green eyes wide with vulnerability.

"I love you."

"You couldn't lead with *that?*" I challenged.

She'd amazed me with this news about her being pregnant. As soon as she told me that we would be having a baby, I struggled to breathe through the shock. I felt struck. Knocked over. Blown away. The concept that she was going to be the mother of my child was such a large one that I lagged to accept it.

It sounded too good to be true.

It seemed like I'd wanted it for so long that now that it was happening, I had to shift my mind all over again. And open up my heart that much more.

Once her arms were free, she looped them over my back.

I slammed my mouth to hers, tasting the salt of her tears. She mewled, parting her lips as she breathed into me and kissed me for all she was worth. Pushing against me, she poured her affections into the gesture, and my already hard dick ached even more to be inside her.

"I love you," she repeated as I held her close, reveling in her naked, warm presence that molded so perfectly against me.

"I love this baby, and I am so shocked and happy that we can have one."

I kissed her again and brushed back her red tresses to peer into her turbulent gaze. "Why wouldn't you be happy?"

"I…" She sighed, clinging to me as I hugged her closer, lying on my side to face her.

"I never wanted a child before. When I knew my life would be nothing more than working on Mom's farm and making as much money as I could to care for her, I didn't want to bring a new life into that hardship. But now that I've found you and realized how much I could love you, from the bottom of my heart, I am excited about the future, not worried. At least I'm not worried about this child's future. He or she will have the best dad."

Her slow, shy smile killed me. Her tender kiss melted my heart.

"And a present mom who will always acknowledge him or her." She grinned, confident to express how much she'd love our child.

I held her tightly, kissing her as I prompted her to roll with me. With her body draped over mine, her arms around my neck and my hands secured over her ass, I moaned at the heat of her bare pussy over my erection.

"And a doting grandmother."

She leaned up and frowned.

I wished I could say our baby would have a grandfather, too, but I wasn't optimistic that Dad would last that long.

"What?" She shook her head. "I... I don't understand. Your mother passed away long ago, and my mom..."

"Will soon be healthy and hardy to welcome her grandchild into this world too."

She opened her eyes wide. "What do you mean?"

"I took over all her debt." It was nothing, a chunk of change with my wealth, but it meant a world of difference to her. "I visited her doctors and the staff in charge of her care. She's doing fine with the slight respiratory infection that landed her in the hospital. So fine that she didn't hesitate to warn me that I must treat her one and only daughter well."

Gaping at me, she seemed unable to move.

"She clearly learned her lesson about mixing with Mob men." I grunted a laugh, unable to resist touching my wife. Up and down, I rubbed my hands over her ass cheeks as I explained. "She wanted to know what I was there for, and I told her all of it. That you'd married me to pay off her debts. That Shane lied to you."

She swallowed hard. "*All* of it?"

I nodded. "All of it. She was protective, worried about you with someone like me, but I explained that you weren't 'mixing' with me or having a fling like she had with your father. I made sure she understood that you are my wife." I pulled her down for a hard, sound kiss, earning a sexy mewl. "And you will be my wife until we both grow old together and die."

She dipped low to kiss me harder.

"I've taken on her bills, and she will receive her kidney transplant next week. As soon as she is cleared from this respiratory concern, she will be transported for the surgery."

"Declan…" She lowered to kiss me again, slow and sweet. "I don't know how to ever thank you."

I chuckled, rubbing her ass and reveling in her soft skin. "Thank me?"

She nodded.

"You don't have to thank me. I'm your husband. You are my family."

Again, she laid her lips on mine. I gripped her ass and pulled her down on me.

Sitting up abruptly, she tugged my pants off, and I removed my shirt.

But I didn't want her to resort to sex just yet. It was a foolproof way for us to be close and connect, but I wasn't finished explaining.

As she straddled me, kissing me and rubbing her moist pussy over me, I held back and growled.

"You are my wife, Cara. And I wish you could understand how much you matter to be able to tell me all of that."

She sighed against my lips, pressing her weight to my dick. "I *did* tell you."

"Later," I argued.

"I was too scared to tell you sooner. I didn't know... I wasn't aware that I could love you so much. That we would click and make sense like this." She cut herself off, kissing me again as she ground over me.

"And once I realized that you had my heart, I did tell you, because I hated to think of hurting you or deceiving you."

I exhaled a long breath of relief. Those sweet, sincere words meant the world to me.

"Do you understand now, Cara?"

She raised her brows.

"Do you understand that I love you?" I angled my dick up toward her entrance, sliding in slowly.

Her head hung down. Her auburn tresses curtained her face, and with a slow push back, she sank over my hardness.

"I love you, Cara." I promised it with a kiss, and she dragged out her retreat, lifting off me until just the tip remained.

"I fucking love everything about you," I growled, squeezing her ass as she rode me slowly. "And I will always do everything I can to make you happy."

She hummed, smiling lazily. "Oh, I'm very happy with you like this."

I lowered my lids, looking up at her with pure contentment. "I can tell."

"I want to make love with you," she purred as she slid down me all the way.

The tight suction of her pussy was perfection, but I let her take charge for once. "Why did you tell me to stop earlier?"

"I was afraid you'd be rough."

I squeezed her ass tighter. "I thought you liked it rough." Teasing her with my finger along her ass crack, I watched as her expression changed to a hotter degree of desire.

"I do."

Holding her up, I replaced my dick with my finger, gathering her cream to lube up my push into her ass. She didn't want that, readjusting until she wrapped around my dick again.

Slow, but steady, I played with her ass as she rode me.

"I... I didn't want to be rough with the baby."

I grinned, loving how worried and careful she already was. She would be an excellent mother. I already knew she was a perfect wife and an amazing lover.

"Harder," she begged.

I added another finger, still careful to be slow and easy.

We came together, and she sagged in my arms as I carried her to the shower. In the stall, I held her close, never wanting to be far from her again.

"I can't believe you went to see my mom," she admitted.

I kissed her brow, rinsing the shampoo out of her hair. "That was why I was gone. I had to do things right by you."

"For two days?"

I loved that she'd counted down the time.

"I stopped at the Murray residence first."

She angled back, giving me a stern look. "Why?"

"Don't worry about it."

Still, she was curious. "Is... he alive?"

I chuckled, loving that she could be just as dark to wish him dead. "Trust me. Making them pay back every cent of debt and more will be a worse punishment than the mercy of death."

I felt her cheek rise in a smile against my chest as I held her again.

"Then I was at the hospital. Ian has been handling a lot of it. He's the diplomatic one between us. I had him begin the process of paying for it all."

"All that administrative headache," she said, sighing.

"Yes. Once Nora is healthy enough to travel after the kidney transplant, she can move here."

Again, she jerked back to face me. "*What?*"

I would never get tired of surprising her and spoiling her. In bed and out of it.

"If that is what you want. And what she wants," I added. Having a complete family here would be nice. If I had to dictate the future, we were only getting started.

"She'll be eager to meet her grandbaby." I furrowed my brow. "Which reminds me."

"What?" She looped her arms around me, and I relished her loose embrace.

"She was protective. So much so that she was blunt to put me on the spot and ask whether I'd married you just to knock you up."

She frowned.

That had been the plan. And that plan got screwed up along the way.

"Why would she think you could be knocked up?"

Cara shook her head. "I have no clue."

"And what also doesn't make sense is the lack of medical notes from anything that indicated that you'd lost an ovary during surgery."

"How would you know?"

I smirked. "Cara. I make people talk. I move papers. I say get it done and it gets done." How else did she think I'd taken over her mother's medical care so easily?

"I tasked Ian with finding all your medical history. I wanted to know how slim the odds were with you."

She kissed my chest. "If the chances of my fertility were that low, would you have left me?"

I rolled my eyes. "Letting you go was never an option."

Her mouth dropped open. "But we shook on it!" She smiled, laughing.

I shrugged. "I lied. And no." I leaned down to kiss her. "If you had slim chances of fertility, we'd keep trying. Forever. I want you, and only you, to be the mother of my children."

She smiled up at me.

"Ian has yet to find any record of your enduring a surgery that would complicate your fertility. And when your mother seemed to think otherwise…"

Furrowing her brow, she seemed pensive and confused. "I don't get it. When I had pain in my back and stomach, Mom rushed me to the city. The clinic near the farm wasn't equipped for too much, and that was the one time she'd insisted on my father paying for anything for me."

I nodded. "Right. There is a document of your having an appendectomy. But nothing more."

She narrowed her eyes. "Then why was I told I'd lost an ovary and…?"

"*Who* told you that?"

Her face turned stony. "Keira. My father suggested that she stand in and talk to the nurses and doctors instead of 'troubling' him or me. My mom had to go back to the farm. It bothered her not to be there, but she had to make things work to count on our livelihood to continue."

It was making more sense now.

"Keira had to have fudged the truth. Made up the stuff about my ovaries and whatnot." She shook her head, growling lightly. "That *bitch*!"

She did it out of spite, I was sure. Just to hurt Cara.

"We'll make sure you have the best medical care now. You and the baby both," I promised as I cupped her face and kissed her tenderly.

Now that we'd found each other, I would never let anything stand in the way of ensuring that she was happy and healthy.

And with me. Forever.

30

CARA

One year later...

Donal smiled as soon as my mother picked him up. I rolled my eyes, smirking at his biggest source of being spoiled.

"Mom."

"Oh, hush," she chided. "He's just too darned cute to let suffer."

"He wasn't suffering. He needs to get more used to being on his tummy." I couldn't be mad. Seeing my mother healthy and happy, holding my son, would always make my heart swell with love and joy.

She'd put on some weight, and every day that she lived here, she seemed less like that shell of disease and weakness from before.

"Aren't you?" she cooed at him, carrying him away and swaying as she hummed an old lullaby I recalled her using on me when I was younger.

"Again?" Riley laughed as she came into the room. She shook her head, smiling at my mother. "That boy's never going to want to do tummy time if she saves him from it nonstop."

I laughed at the cook. She'd become more of a friend than a member of the staff. Over the last year, I'd welcomed my role in the household. As the wife of a Mob lord. The mother of an heir. And the woman at the head of the castle the guards would do well to listen to.

Running wasn't an option. It never had been. But right now, as I realized my mother could keep my three-month-old preoccupied, I wanted to run into my husband's arms.

He'd come home just moments ago, and I was eager for a chance to talk with him.

And explore his rugged body.

Having my mother here was a blessing, but I still wished Donal could have met his namesake.

Declan and Ian's father passed away three months before his grandson was born, but I was glad he'd had a chance to know he was coming soon.

After Declan and I confessed our love for each other, he took me up to the blocked-off floor and introduced me to his father. He was weak and gruff, but as soon as I learned that he was the one who spent so much time building up the impressive stables out back, I quickly bonded with him. Then when my mother moved in, she'd kept him company talking about horses too.

Oscar took over the farm I'd worked so hard to keep going. At first, I worried that Mom would struggle to give it up. Her love for me, and the excitement about having a grandchild, was plenty to persuade her to sell the farm to Oscar.

Declan practically gave it away, selling it for next to nothing because he felt that it was a repayment to the stable hand for always being there for me when my own father hadn't been. With new equipment, rebuilt barns, and actual staff, Oscar was set to be very successful. He often visited, glad to check out the lands here and ride out with me, Mom, or Declan.

He'd become a family friend, not an employee, and I was glad it had worked out so well.

After Donal passed away, Mom split her time between helping me prepare for the baby and at the stables. That was how I cut my time too. Although I was a new mother, I was young, and there was so much to enjoy and do with the stables here. Breeding plans were in place, and I was eager to see how the stables would grow with my influence.

Unfortunately, after Donal passed away, Ian grew distant. Declan worried about him. My gruff husband seemed to always be worried or concerned about something or the other.

Being the head of the head of the Sullivan Family was no small role to fulfill. But he was just the man for it, always quick to act and level headed enough to rule.

I knew he noticed how Ian had pulled away. I was curious about it too. I'd gotten slightly closer to my brother-in-law, and I was happy to see him enjoy being an uncle, but what if it wasn't just grief? What if he was bothered about something other than losing his father?

Motherhood was a blessing, even though it was hard. And fitting into my role in this family and household was a constant challenge too. Now, it was one I welcomed.

Yet, when I spotted Declan heading upstairs, on his phone, I hustled after him. I was determined for him to take me to bed, to spend time with me, not all the issues of the week.

I caught up to him just outside our room, but I didn't surprise him. It was almost impossible to ever actually catch him unaware. Trained and skilled as a fighter, he had to be quick like that.

As I reached up to pull his phone down from whatever he was texting, he caught me in his arms and heaved me up over his shoulder. It wasn't often that he loosened up to be this playful, but I loved it when he was.

"Trying to sneak up on me?" he teased.

I giggled, reaching around his waist to unbutton his pants as he carried me into our room and shut the door.

"Sort of."

He grunted a laugh, setting me down on my feet. I resumed taking off his pants, eager to have my way with him. "What's the hurry?"

"I don't know when I'll get another chance to do this with you," I teased back.

With his pants gone, I dropped to kiss up along his shaft.

"Oh, it's *my* fault?" He sighed and rocked up to my face. "You're the one doing too much."

I rolled my eyes, sucking him in.

"If you're not busy at the stables, you're busy with Donal."

I hummed, laving his veiny length.

"And if you're not handling the household, you're catching up with your mother."

His hands cupped my face, and I gazed up at him with his cock stuffed in my mouth. "I've been meaning to have a talk with you about overworking yourself, wife of mine."

"Well," I said after he pulled out of my mouth and picked me up to set me on the bed, "I like to stay busy."

He pulled my clothes off, kissing my flesh as he exposed it. "I'll keep you busy here."

I grinned. "You have to remind me when I overdo it," I said. "I get too worked up on controlling every little thing and get ahead of myself."

"I know," he agreed, lying with me. "And I will do better." He sighed against my skin as he trailed hot, wet kisses down the sides of my breasts.

"This week has been a long one," he added.

"Aren't they *all* long?"

He teased my nipple, staring up at me. "I had to deal with your father."

I tensed. "Way to kill a mood there, Declan."

He grinned, slipping his fingers in me and getting me right back on track with my arousal.

"Do I want to know?" I asked, not too far gone with him to maintain a conversation.

"Keira tried to have him killed."

No way.

"She put a hit on him?"

"Yes. It seems that he wanted to pull the same stunt he pulled with you. He arranged Saoirse in a marriage with someone Keira hated, all so he could get some easy money."

I shook my head, smiling.

Over the winter, they'd lost it all. The mansion went up on the market and failed to sell. Jewelry, clothes, designer crap, and cars. They pawned it all to pay Declan back, and the last I heard from Ian, they were nowhere close to being able to clear that debt.

"He planned to have Saoirse be Smith's bride."

I laughed, amused when he chuckled too.

"He's, like, ninety years old!"

"I had to intervene. I don't need anyone killing off your father. He's going to live the longest life possible, miserable every minute he has to pay me back." He stared at me, hungry and wicked as he considered how I opened wide for him.

"Enough talking," I begged at the sinister intention in his eyes.

"Hmm, you think?" He reached up for the drawers. That motion usually meant that he wanted to tie me up or play rougher than usual.

"Not tonight," I said.

"No?" He arched a brow.

I loved his darkness. I thrived when he was rough and hard with me. Under his careful balance, I could rely on that hit of pain to result in the best blessing of bliss. His dominance was the ultimate turn-on, and I loved that he knew it too.

It didn't matter whether we were in the bedroom or not, he always knew how to appease me and see to my every carnal need. If I'd never met him, if I hadn't thought twice about marrying him, I never would have known this sweet release. I never would've been welcomed to this raw passion that I needed from a hard man like him.

Declan took my virginity my wedding night, and he had done so violently. It was my introduction to sex, and it was only under his dominating treatment that I learned what I liked. He was my first, and would be my last, and it was because of him that I realized I liked it hard. That I enjoyed it when he pushed me. Tied me up. Spanked me. Even fucked my ass.

I never would have known that about myself without him.

And I *never* shied away from his darkness, craving it instead.

"Why not tonight?" he asked, crawling back over me and teasing me with his erection poking at my stomach. He lowered more, lining up to enter me.

"It just might not be a bad idea to go easy on me," I said lightly.

I didn't know if he'd make the connection. The last time I'd voiced my concerns about his taking me too roughly was that night when I told him I was pregnant with our son. When I told him that I loved him and when he confessed the same to me.

The doctors and midwife assured me that sex was fine. Even a harder level of intimacy. Declan and I compromised, making sure we were comfortable and sated, but he knew that I worried about carrying a child.

He had been right. Keira finally admitted that she'd lied to me about my supposed infertility issues. Soon after word got out about us expecting our first son, she'd made a nasty comment and ended up coming clean. She'd only done so to try to hurt me further, but I didn't care.

I was over the moon that she was wrong, and I'd spend the rest of my life having a family with my husband.

Declan smiled, staying deep inside me without moving. "You want me to go easy on you tonight?"

I smiled wider and nodded.

"Are you...?" His brows shot up high. "You're pregnant? Again? So soon?"

The excitement and joy in his tone thrilled me.

I nodded again. "It looks like we're going to have Irish twins, my love."

After his search to secure an heir, I was well ahead of the game.

"I fucking love you," he growled.

I kissed him back as he filled me, knowing my heart would never stop swelling with adoration for this hard Mob man.

Printed in Great Britain
by Amazon